1972

This book may be kept

"WE

NEVER

MAKE

MISTAKES"

TWO SHORT NOVELS

By Alexander Solzhenitsyn

"WE

NEVER

MAKE

MISTAKES"

*Translated from the Russian
and with an introduction*

By Paul W. Blackstock

UNIVERSITY OF SOUTH CAROLINA PRESS
COLUMBIA   1963

CONTENTS

v

Translator's Preface

The difficulties encountered in translating contemporary Russian are too well-known to require elaboration. They illustrate only too well the familiar Italian proverb, *traduttore-traditore* (the translator is a traitor). An attempt has been made to retain as much of the flavor of the original as possible in colloquial American English without sacrificing accuracy. Thus for those who may prefer to read the original without use of a dictionary the present translation is literal enough to serve as a useful guide. Unfamiliar abbreviations, such as NKPS (People's Commissariat of Communication Routes) are explained as they occur in the text in brackets. Words which are left in the original Russian, such as *izba* (peasant hut or cottage), are handled in the same manner. Familiar abbreviations, such as NKVD (State Security, i.e. secret police) are left without explanation. A brief glossary of important and/or recurrent terms in the order of their occurrence is appended below.

I am indebted to Mrs. Dorothy Hanson, Professor of Russian at Columbia College, Columbia, South Carolina, for a first-draft literal translation of the Krechetovka Station story, and to Professor Samuel Pevsner of Washington, D. C., for invaluable assistance with unclean and difficult words in both stories. Like others who studied Russian under Prof. Pevsner while serving in the Pentagon, I am indebted to him for his patience, his stimulating teaching, and his encouragement to continue private study after leaving public service. Mrs. Elizabeth Legzdins of New York was helpful in translating certain peasant expressions and vocabulary. But above all, I am indebted for linguistic advice and assistance to Leon Volkov, contributing editor on Russian Affairs of *Newsweek* magazine, and his wife Galina, who reviewed the final draft of both stories; and to Abraham Brumberg, executive editor of the U. S. I. A. journal, *Problems of Communism,* who reviewed the Introduction. Finally, sincere appreciation is due to Mrs. Cloris Grogan, secretary of the Institute of International Studies here at the University of South Carolina, who typed the manuscript from a very difficult final draft. Also I wish to thank Mrs. Catharine Rembert of the University's Art Department, who made the sketches based on original Soviet source materials.

Paul W. Blackstock

Introduction

Alexander Solzhenitsyn's "Two Stories" appeared in the January, 1963, issue of the Soviet literary magazine, *Novy Mir* (New World), which had previously published his sensational story of life in the Stalinist labor camps, *One Day in the Life of Ivan Denisovich.* In a foreword to this earlier work, Alexander Tvardovsky, Editor-in-Chief of *Novy Mir,* wrote that "it marks the appearance on the literary scene of a new, original and mature talent." He had such a feeling of gratitude for the honesty and candor of Solzhenitsyn's work that his "greatest wish" was that "this gratitude be shared by other readers." Hence the publication of these "Two Stories," or two short novels.

To the reader who lives in an open, unregimented society, this kind of remark may seem puzzling. What, one may ask, is so unusual about appearance of a new Soviet author who writes openly and honestly about life as he has known it? And why should the Soviet reader be grateful for the opportunity to read his works?

There are no simple, direct answers to these questions. The explanation lies deep in the nature of Soviet society and the role which the artist, especially the writer, is called upon to play in it.

The impression created by the Soviet system on the visitor from one of our open, Western societies is one of "togetherness gone mad." The state has created an official ideal image of Soviet society as a sort of grandiose, prize-winning collective in which each private individual heroically overfulfills his plan, no matter how great the obstacles.

For example, in their first-grade reader, all Soviet school children are introduced to an ideal image of "Mother" drawn for them in a story which begins: "My mother works in a factory and makes little electric lamps. Every month she overfulfills the plan." A Marxist-Leninist ideology and an official image of Soviet life and society are thus imposed on the individual beginning in his earliest formative years.

All must pay lip service to these concepts, and, under the doctrine of Socialist Realism, artists are called upon to reinforce them. They are regarded by the state as instruments in the general task of uplifting and indoctrinating Soviet society, and, what is more, are for the most part willing to accept this role. This is especially true of writers, whom Soviet Chairman N. S. Khrushchev, addressing the Fourth Congress of the Union of Soviet writers in May, 1959, described as "a type of artillery. They clear the way for our forward movement, and help our Party in the Communist education of workers." He added, with typical Khrushchevian candor, "You must brainwash the people with your works!"

This is the official literary mission. The doctrine of Socialist Realism has been developed not only to defend this mission, but as a means of condemning all art which, according to official standards, fails to provide the necessary uplift, to sound a call to overfulfill the plan, and to portray life as part of the ever-forward march of Soviet collectivism, which is implicitly held up as the ultimate goal of all humanity.

Since the death of Stalin and the publication in 1954 of Ilya Ehrenberg's novel, *The Thaw,* followed by Vladimir Dudintsev's *Not By Bread Alone,* there has been a tentative unfreezing of the rigid Socialist Realism formula. A random sample of recent Soviet novels and short stories will reveal both the strengths and weaknesses of literature produced under these somewhat improved conditions.

The uninitiated reader is both attracted and repelled by current

x

Soviet literature. He is attracted by the fact that many of the authors have talent. Obviously they can produce what by Western standards would be called good — perhaps even great — literature, until the inevitable Communist indoctrination seeps through. The social and political lessons are rarely subtle. In most cases they are as obtrusive as the ubiquitous hammer-and-sickle symbol of Soviet power. Certainly the Western reader, and probably many Soviet citizens as well, find this continuous moralizing and political indoctrination both repulsive and disheartening. What a pity that such talents are employed (or in some cases clearly prostituted) for purely didactic or propaganda purposes!

At least two features are common to most current Soviet writing and image-making. First, work — almost any kind of work as long as it is hard and unremitting — is held up as one of the highest individual and collective ideals. Theoretically it is not only an end in itself which gives life meaning, but is also richly rewarded. As a general rule, manual labor is highly romanticized, above all, tireless, "heroic," labor in a pioneer setting, as illustrated by Alexis Malenkii's long novel, *Developers of the Tundra* (Pokoriteli Tundry) — (*Siberskie Ogni*, 1959-60). Thus a large percentage of Soviet short stories and novels falls into what may be called the "production" or "construction" category or genre. Second, the Communist Party and the collective organizations under its influence or control are idealized and romanticized. These range from individual work brigades to collective farms and large Party or bureaucratic institutions. Frequently a story line will concentrate on the individual human being, caught in circumstances beyond his control by an unkind fate, who is miraculously rescued by the Party or by one of its organizations.

He thus achieves "true happiness" in the collective, as illustrated in a story, very skillfully drafted, by Boris Zubavin, entitled "Happiness" (Radost) — (*Moskva*, 1962). It should be noted that in the Soviet moral universe this kind of happiness is the equivalent of "salvation" for the Christian. The basic Western idea that "no man is an island" has been distorted beyond all recognition. The ideal prototype of the new Soviet man achieves inner grace by selfless toil, but his redemption can only come from the collective, when at the decisive moment of his life's struggle, he merges with it and "measures up to the demands of the Revolution, of human society, of history."

The strength of such literature lies in its idealism and optimism. Its writers, frequently with undeniable skill and talent, accomplish the mission laid down for them by the canons of Socialist Realism.

They discharge what a Soviet youth recently called:

> that great responsibility which has been placed upon our generation — to preserve the fire of the October Revolution, not to surrender a single position, to rise yet another step in man's ascent toward the sun, toward happiness, toward light. [Stormy applause.]
>
> (*Komsomolskaya Pravda*, April 5, 1961.)

Soviet writers who accomplish such tasks (or indeed, any who are published at all) are well paid for their work.

Such writing has its counterpart in many of the Horatio Alger, success story novels produced in the open, unregimented societies of the West. The "happy-ending" formula literature of the West — like its Soviet counterpart — also pays its producers well. In this genre some readers may be inclined to rate Soviet writing (which at least has a well-defined set of social objectives) higher than purely escapist literature which offers no goal other than the aimless pursuit of pleasure in an idealized affluence—utterly beyond the reach of the majority of the people. Some readers may also prefer Soviet "uplift" literature to Western products of various "realistic" schools, which apparently regard almost any parade of sex and violence as Art, especially if the product is infused with elements of social protest.

When queried as to "why they do it?", writers who specialize in the *Rebecca of Sunnybrook Farm* or *Developers of the Tundra* product come up with the counterquestion: "After all, we have to eat, don't you agree?" Talleyrand had an unkind but pertinent reply:

"I don't see the necessity." The pity of it all, as far as Soviet authors are concerned, is that basically there is no market for any other kind of product. There is only one publisher — the State. The "work conquers all" type of story is what the Government wants and what it buys. There are no private presses, although a few hand-mimeographed poems or stories are occasionally circulated surreptitiously.

The weaknesses of literature produced by the Socialist Realism formula are too familiar to require extensive elaboration here. As with all the products of "formula" writing, whether capitalist or Soviet, the characters are simply not human. They are stylized caricatures of human beings which move like puppets through a distorted dreamworld. Both the Rover Boys and the heroic figures of the Soviet "production" novels are equally hollow, equally out of touch with the real world.

The basic weakness has been recognized in rare moments of candor by official Soviet sources themselves. For example, *Komsomolskaya Pravda,* the daily paper of the Young Communist League, in its April 5, 1961, issue, quoted the following candid criticism by a young teacher from the Leningrad State Pedagogical Institute:

> The heroes of our literature and of our theatre merely hint at what we see in real life. There is no arguing that our young people have courage and other fine qualities. But whenever we try to show a hero personifying these qualities — say, a builder on a construction site or in the virgin lands — what emerges is something rather schematic, sometimes even grotesque.

This criticism strikes home, as anyone with the patience to read through a representative sampling of contemporary Soviet literature can testify. It is precisely because such "heroic" literature is so far out of touch with reality — either human or Soviet — that the editor of *Novy Mir,* quoted above, is grateful for the kind of direct, honest portrayal of life found in Solzhenitsyn's earlier work, and in the "Two Stories" translated here. Millions of Soviet readers and others abroad will undoubtedly share that gratitude.

There is nothing sensational about these "Two Stories" except that they were written as literature, i.e., for their own sake. The first, "An Incident at Krechetovka Station," merely describes a typical day at a provincial railroad station during a critical period in the early days of World War II. An unfortunate straggler from a military unit, a former Moscow actor, is denounced by an over-zealous station commandant, who later has some gnawing second thoughts about his action. The situation is familiar to millions in the Soviet Union and in formerly Nazi-occupied Europe who have known life under a police-state regime. Even the moral of the story — if there must be one according to the rules of the game — is fully in line with N. S. Khrushchev's concluding recommendation in his address to the Twenty-second Congress: "It is our duty to go carefully into all aspects of all matters concerned with the abuse of power. . . . This must be done to prevent such things from happening in the future."

The second story, "Matryona's House," has even less plot and action than the first. Apparently it is partly autobiographical, but the story is essentially a character sketch of an aging woman in typical Russian peasant surroundings — a squalid *izba* (a one-room peasant hut or cottage) at the edge of a tiny settlement, with her lame cat, scraggly goat, and a lodger, the local schoolteacher who tells the story, and who in 1953, a few months after Stalin's death, returns from ten years of exile in Soviet Central Asia. By a striking coincidence the principal character, Matryona Vasilyevna, when introduced to modern music by way of her tenant's radio, rejects the singing of Chaliapin, the famous Russian baritone, for the songs of Glinka. As recently as March, 1963, N. S. Khrushchev, in a speech censoring formalism in the arts, told Party leaders, writers, and artists that "Whenever I listen to Glinka, tears of joy come to my eyes." In this regard, at least, "Matryona's House" should meet with the approval of the regime's foremost critic.

What emerges from both these stories is an unforgettable picture of what Russian life — or at least an important segment of it —

is really like. They are in the great tradition of the stories of peasant life written by Turgenev and Tolstoy — stories which contributed materially to the prerevolutionary scene in late nineteenth- and early twentieth-century Russia. They have the same ring of authenticity, pay a similar attention to significant detail, and provide comparable insights into Russian character.

In his March 1963 speech to the Soviet writers and artists, Khrushchev forcefully indicated that the liberal trend in art and literature had gone too far, and that it was time to retreat back into the rigid framework of Socialist Realism. Although Khrushchev mentioned Solzhenitsyn's work favorably, there were rumors in Moscow that Tvardovsky, editor of *Novy Mir,* who published it, would be removed from his post. The rumors proved false, but the March issue of *Novy Mir* appeared a month late, and the last installment of Ilya Ehrenberg's controversial memoirs was much shorter than previous ones. The young poet Yevtushenko's planned visit to the United States was canceled. On the other hand, three Soviet writers (Alexander Yessenin-Volpin, Michael Naritza, Valeriy Tsaris) who had formerly been declared insane and forcibly detained in insane asylums, were quietly released.

All these signs point to a campaign against liberalism similar to the one which took place in 1957 after publication abroad of the late Boris Pasternak's prize-winning novel, *Doctor Zhivago.* How far the current "refreeze" will go and how long it will last is an open question, part of the larger problem of how any authoritarian regime handles the emergence of an art and literature of social protest, a subject which merits brief consideration.

It is ironic that the Soviet regime has nursed its present generation of intellectuals on the social protest literature of Western Europe and the United States. Today, forty-five per cent of all Soviet grade school students study English as a second language continuously for six or seven years. In the course of even such elementary instruction the Russian student actually reads more English and American literature than American students at the same grade level. Certainly, most contemporary Russian authors are familiar with outstanding examples of social protest writing ranging from the novels of Dickens and Mark Twain through Dreiser, Faulkner, Steinbeck, and England's "Angry Young Men" of today. (The study of such literature is encouraged since presumably it "unmasks" or exposes the evils and contradictions theoretically inherent in a bourgeois capitalist system which, according to dialectical materialism, makes its ultimate replacement by Communist society inevitable. It is hoped the Soviet student will form an image of the United States, for example, which is a composite of *An American Tragedy, Tobacco Road,* and *Grapes of Wrath.*) Moreover, many of the great Russian classics of the nineteenth century were written in protest against the obvious political and social abuses of the Czarist regime. Under these circumstances it is inevitable that Russian intellectuals writing today should seek some means of protesting against similar abuses which they discern in contemporary Soviet society. However, by definition the Soviet system has none of the weaknesses of previous, capitalist societies and is a near-Utopia in transition to the final Marxist Paradise. Accordingly, the regime attempts to contain the writer's deep-seated urge to protest within the increasingly inadequate doctrinal framework of Socialist Realism. Ever since the 1956 Twentieth Party Congress when de-Stalinization became official policy, the regime has permitted criticism of the Stalinist past. The abuses of that period can be attributed to "the cult of the individual" and have theoretically been corrected with the new course under Khrushchev. For a significant number of "angry" Russians of all ages, however, this minor concession has not been enough. They have sent abroad, for publication under assumed names, works which protest against present abuses. The most familiar example is Abram Tertz's (pseudonym) *The Trial Begins.* For the moment the regime has responded by another official warning from Khrushchev and certain repressive measures. But like open terror (which Khrushchev has denounced as a Stalinist crime) such repressive measures have their limits, and ultimately prove self-defeating. Too many bullets put an end to all cooperation. Similarly, artists and authors cannot fulfill their assigned tasks from jails or insane asylums. Some sort of compromise is called for and may take the already established form of an increasingly flexible interpretation of what is permissible under Socialist Realism.

The USSR has made enormous scientific and technological progress in the last decade since no more than lip service to dialectical materialism is now required of Russian scientists. This is an encouraging sign of growing intellectual honesty and maturity, and if the trend is extended to the humanities, the USSR may yet come of age and take its rightful place among the truly civilized powers in the society of nations. Now that the Soviets have demonstrated that they are no longer "backward" in science and technology, they may seek to demonstrate that they are a *kulturny* (cultured) nation as well. A first step in this direction would be to show enough self-confidence in their much vaunted "new Soviet society" to permit the free development of a literature of social protest. Obviously the present Soviet leadership lacks this self-confidence. However, a hesitant first step in the direction of cultural emancipation has already been taken with the publication of novels and stories such as these by Solzhenitsyn which are written as literature rather than for the lessons they contain.

It is encouraging that Soviet authorities have permitted the publication of such writing, under the claim that "today there is no aspect of our life that cannot be dealt with and faithfully described in Soviet literature." Let us hope that this claim may yet be proven true, that the regime will someday permit its authors to return to the original sources of Russian inspiration, to the Russian people and to the Russian soil, which somehow stubbornly resists political indoctrination. It may be that with increasing maturity, the USSR, now widely recognized as one of the superpowers in the world today, will outgrow some of its youthful preoccupation with purely political objectives. It may even be that Russia will again return to the main stream of Western civilization. However, one swallow does not make a spring.

On the one hand, the appearance of such stories as these of Solzhenitsyn could mark the beginning of a new flowering of Russian literature. On the other hand, such promising new efforts could be suppressed and the men who produced them could be silenced in a new wave of tyranny and oppression. The latter development is unlikely at this stage under the present Soviet regime. On the contrary, the persistent demand for more, rather than less, artistic freedom is already so strong that it is doubtful whether a narrow strait jacket of Socialist Realism can in fact be reimposed on Soviet literature by those who, like the Stalinist security police, "never make mistakes."

Paul W. Blackstock

Columbia, South Carolina

May, 1963

GLOSSARY

Da: The Russian word for "yes" or frequently "O.K."

"Heated," warm or converted cars: These were boxcars adapted for troop transport.

Izba: Russian one-room peasant hut or cottage, usually with a thatched roof, and frequently attached to a second larger room or *gornitza* (as in the case of Matryona's house).

NKVD: Soviet State Security Police, i.e., secret police.

Stragglers: At the time of the Nazi onslaught in 1941, literally hundreds of thousands of Russian troops were encircled or surrounded; others were lost or escaped. The word straggler is used to refer to all such persons, whether civilian or military.

Tchkalov - V.P.: Soviet pilot and officer who flew nonstop from Moscow to Vancouver, B. C., in 1937 and died in military service in December 1938, honored as a Soviet "Lindbergh."

Turgenev - I.S.: Nineteenth century Russian novelist famous for stories of peasant life, *A Sportsman's Sketches* and novels such as *Fathers and Sons* and *Virgin Soil.*

Gornitza: The large, unused second room of Matryona's house attached to the *izba* or hut proper — valuable for its logs and roof.

Belinsky, Panferov: V. G. Belinski, Nineteenth century Russian critic; F. I. Panferov, Soviet author whose novel *Borbaza mir* won a Stalin Prize in 1948.

Nanya or *lyolka*: Nannie or nurse, a familiar term of endearment.

An Incident

at

Krechetovka Station

"Hello. Is this the dispatcher?"

"Well?"

"Who is this? Dyachichin?"

"Well?"

"Don't 'well' me — I said, are you Dyachichin?"

"Drive the tank car from track seven to three. Yes, I'm Dyachichin."

"This is the Army Commandant's aide, Lieutenant Zotov, speaking! Listen, what're you doing up there? Why haven't you dispatched the echelon to Lipetsk before this? Number 67—uh—what's the last number, Valya?"

"Eight."

"No, 678."

"There's nothing to pull it with."

"What do you mean, 'nothing to pull it with?' "

"There are no engines—so—Varnakoff? Varnakoff! Do you see four flatcars of coal there on track six? Well, pull them here."

"Listen, if there are no engines, why can I see six of them lined up from my window?"

"Those are couplers."

"What . . . couplers?"

"For engines. From the graveyard. They're evacuating."

"Good! Then you have two switch engines moving!"

1

"Comrade Lieutenant? About the yard engines, I saw . . . three!"

"Right here beside me is the convoy commander of this transport echelon, he'll set me straight . . . There are three switch engines. Let me have one of them!"

"I can't."

"What do you mean, you 'can't?' Do you realize the importance of this cargo? It mustn't be delayed one minute, and you—"

"Drive it up the mound."

". . . and you've already held it up almost twelve hours!"

"Oh, not twelve hours."

"What are you running there — a nursery school or a dispatcher's office? Why are all those children screaming?"

"Because they crowd into the place. Comrade, how many times must I tell you? Clean up the room! I can't dispatch anyone in this mess. Even an Army cargo would have to stay."

"But this echelon has a shipment of preserved blood! For the hospitals! Understand?"

"I understand everything. Varnakov? Now, take off — go to the watering station and take ten."

"Listen — if in the next half-hour you don't dispatch this echelon, I'll notify your superiors! No joke! You'll answer for this!"

"Vasili Vasilitch! Give me the telephone — I myself —"

"I'm handing this over to the Army dispatcher."

"Nickolai Petrovitch? This is Podshebyakina. What's going on at your depot? You know, only the Medical Directorate train was refueled."

"Da, Comrade Sergeant, go to the convoy, and if in forty minutes — No, if by 6:30 you haven't been released — you will come back and report yourself."

"Yes, sir, come back and report to you. May I leave?"

"You may go."

The leader of the convoy turned sharply and with his first step, dropped his hand from his cap and went out.

Lieutenant Zotov adjusted his glasses, increased the sternness of the expression on his not-so-stern face, and looked at the Army dispatcher, Podshebyakina, a young girl in a railroad employee's uniform. Her abundant flaxen curls spilling over her head, she was talking into the old-fashioned mouthpiece of an antiquated telephone. He went from her small room back into his own from which there was no other exit.

The Station Commandant had a corner room on the first floor. Above it, that is, directly above this corner, was a damaged drainpipe. From behind the wall a heavy stream of water was whipped noisily with each blast of the cold wind which took it and splattered it everywhere with a deafening sound — now in front of the left window onto the platform, now in front of the right. After the first clear October frost, when the morning found the whole station covered with white hoarfrost, the weather for these last few days had been soggy. Since yesterday, a cold rain had poured down so hard and so ceaselessly that one wondered where in the whole sky so much water could come from.

On the other hand, the rain also brought with it some order. The stupid and disorderly pushing and shoving of people and the continual swarming of civilians over the platform stopped. These had disturbed the proper appearance and operation of the station. Everybody was hidden from view. No one could be seen crawling under or scrambling over the tops of the cars. There were no local people jostling with buckets of boiled potatoes. The passengers from the freight trains no longer wandered about among the cars with their linens, clothes, and knitted objects hanging all over their arms and shoulders, as if they were going to market. (All this disturbed Lieutenant Zotov. It was not permitted, but he didn't have the heart to prohibit it because rations for the evacuees had not been released.)

Only the people who worked at the station were not driven away by the rain. Through a window a watchman could be seen on the platform near the rain-drenched cargo. Covered with a heavy tarpaulin, he stood there all wet and soaked from the rain without even trying to shake it off. On the third track, the switch engine was slowly moving a tank car, while the switchman, covered entirely

3

with a hooded poncho, waved to him with his flagstick. The dark, dwarfish form of the wagon master could also be seen walking along the train formation on track two, looking and searching under each car.

And so — everything was rain-drenched! In the cold, persistent wind, the rain beat on the roofs and walls of freight cars and the engines. It cut along the fire-red, bent-iron ribs of two, ten-car skeletons (some of the boxes were still burning from the bombing raids, but the useful parts of those remaining had been brought to the rear). It drenched the four Artillery pieces standing on flatcars; it blended with the approaching twilight; it began to tighten and close in on the green, small circle of the semaphore, and on the livid, purple-red sparks which were flying out of the chimneys of the "heated" cars. [These were boxcars adapted for troop transport which in cold weather were fitted with makeshift stoves, with long thin pipes for chimneys that extended through the roof.] All the asphalt on the first platform was covered with crystal-clear water blisters, which had not had time to drain. Even in the dusk the rails glistened and sparkled with bubbles, and all the gray storm covers shimmered with pools of water.

There was little sound besides the trembling of the earth, and the weak sound of the switchman's horn. (Whistling by the engines had been forbidden since the first day of the war.) Only the rain trumpeted through the broken pipes.

Behind the other window of the Commandant's room, in the path along the warehouse enclosure, grew a small oak. Its drenched and trembling branches had held a few dark green leaves, but today even the last few had blown away.

However, there was no time to stand and look around. It was necessary to unroll the masking-paper blinds on the window, light the lamp, and get back to work. Still more important, it was necessary to show some progress before the ten o'clock replacement arrived.

Zotov did not immediately unroll the blinds, but took off his commander's service cap with its green band, which he always wore on duty, even in his room. Tired from the constant copying of the coded numbers of the transports from one list to another, he re-

4

moved his glasses and slowly rubbed his eyes. No, it was not fatigue, but loneliness and weariness that came over him in this darkness before dawn which began to gnaw at him.

His loneliness was not for his wife who, with his unborn child, had remained in faraway White Russia, which was now under German control. It was not for a lost past, because Zotov as yet had none. It was not for a lost fortune, which he never had — and in any case would never want.

Depression gripped Zotov. It stemmed from the need to complain to someone about the course of the war, which was wildly inconceivable to him. From the reports of the Information Bureau he couldn't make out where the front lines were. One could argue about who had taken Kharkhov or who held Kaluga, but among the railroad men it was well known that no trains were being sent through from the Uzlov railroad junction at Tula, and at Eletz they were backed up as far as Berhova. Bombers had penetrated to the Ryazan-Voronezh line, dropping a few bombs here and there, and sometimes hitting even Krechetovka. Ten days ago, from out of nowhere two stray Germans on motorcycles came through Krechetovka, shooting wildly with their machine guns. One of them was killed and the other one got away, and at the station everything was in confusion and disorder. The leader of the special detachment in charge of explosives in case of evacuation, succeeded in pulling away the water-tank car which had been loaded with TNT. He had called in the reconstruction train which had been working there for three days.

What really was bothering Zotov was not the situation at Krechetovka, but why the war was going the way it was. Not only had there not been revolution all over Europe, and not only were we not invading Europe against any combination of aggressors with little loss of life, but look what had happened! How long would this go on? Whatever he did during the day and no matter when he lay down to sleep, Zotov kept thinking: "how long?" Every morning when he was not on duty, but lay sleeping in his apartment, he was awakened by the radio at six o'clock. He woke up hoping that today would come news of victory. But out of the black loud-speaker came forth only hopeless news of the Vyazma and Volokolamsk fronts — and his heart pounded, "Would they even give up Moscow?" he would ask. (Not out loud, it was dangerous to ask this aloud even to himself.) Zotov was afraid to ask this question which he thought about all the time, yet tried hard not to.

But this one dark question was not the last. To give up Moscow would still not end all their misfortunes. Moscow had been given up to Napoleon. It could be burned again, but then what? What if the enemy reached the Urals?

Vasya Zotov felt guilty about even allowing himself to think such shattering thoughts. They were an insult to the all-knowing and all-powerful Father and Teacher — who was always there, who foresaw everything, who took all necessary measures, and who wouldn't permit it.

Some railroad men arrived from Moscow. They had been there in the middle of October, and told of monstrous, unthinkable things — of the flight of factory directors, of the destruction of banks and stores — and silent pain again gripped the heart of Lieutenant Zotov.

Not long ago, on his way here, Zotov had spent two days at the headquarters of the reserve unit. They had thrown a little party, and one very thin and pale young lieutenant with bushy hair had read some of his own poems, which were uncensored and open-hearted. At the time Zotov never thought that he would remember any of the lines, but they kept running through his mind. And now, whether he was walking in Krechetovka, traveling by train to the headquarters of the Commander or by peasant cart to the fortified village Soviet where he had been appointed to give military training to young boys and invalids, Zotov picked out these words and repeated them as his own:

"Our villages are on fire, and our cities all in smoke!
One thought only tortures: When? When?
When can we stop their attack?"

And then there were the lines:

"If in these days Lenin's work falls —
What is there left to live for?"

Since the beginning of the war Zotov had not wanted himself

to be spared. His own little life meant only one thing to him: how much he could help the Revolution. How he had begged to be sent to the front lines! And here he was, stagnating in a railroad command. To be spared for his own sake would be senseless. To be spared for that of his wife and future children — that wouldn't be meaningful either. But if the Germans should reach Lake Baikal and Zotov were still alive — he knew that he would escape, by foot, if necessary, through Kyakhta into China or India, or even across the ocean! He would get away only in order to gather together strong reinforcements and return with arms to Russia and Europe.

And so he stood in the twilight, under the pouring rain which the wind whipped and lashed against the windows. He shivered, and repeated the lines of the young lieutenant's poem.

The darker the room became, the brighter the cherry-red door of the stove appeared, and a spreading yellow sheaf of light fell through the glass window in the door of the adjoining room where the Army dispatcher of the NKPS [Peoples' Commissariat of Communication Routes] then on duty was sitting with the light on.

Although Podshebyakina as an aide on duty was not directly under the Military Commandant, she couldn't perform her duties without him because she was not permitted to know either the contents or the destination of the consignments, only the numbers of the cars. These numbers were brought to her by her helper, who copied them from the cars. Her helper was known as "Aunt Frosia," and was just now entering the room, stamping her feet heavily.

"Ah, this downpour!" she complained. "Ah, this downpour! But it does seem to be lessening a little bit."

"We have to rewrite number 765, Aunt Frosia," said Valya Podshebyakina.

"O.K. I'll write it over. Just let me fix my lantern."

The door wasn't very thick nor was it tightly closed. Zotov could hear their conversation.

"Good, I'll soon receive some coal," Aunt Frosia was saying. "I'm not afraid of anything now. I'll feed the children on some boiled potatoes. But they haven't dug the potatoes up yet at Dashka Milentev's! Just try and dig in that mud!"

"They say it's beginning to frost. It seems to be getting colder."

"It'll be an early winter. Ah, in such a war — we get an early winter! And you, how many potatoes did you dig up?"

Zotov sighed and began pulling down the masking-paper blinds, carefully sealing them to the window frames so no light could be seen from the outside.

This sort of thing was what he couldn't understand, and it brought back his feeling of frustration and loneliness. All these working people around him listened glumly to the news reports, then dispersed from the loud-speakers with the same kind of silent suffering. But Zotov saw a difference. The people around him seemed to live with something besides the news from the front. Some dug the potatoes, some milked the cows, some sawed firewood, and others insulated their windows. And at times these people talked more about these things and busied themselves more with them than with the news from the front.

The foolish old woman! She's got some coal, so now "she isn't afraid of anything!" Not even of Guderian's tanks?

The wind shook the small oak by the warehouse, and in the window of his office a pane trembled.

Zotov unrolled the last window blind and lit the lamp. All at once, in the warm, cleanly swept room, empty but comfortable, there seemed to be more hope, and he began to feel more cheerful.

Directly under the lamp in the middle of the room was a table for the man on duty. Behind Zotov by the stove was a safe. Near the window was an old-fashioned oak station bench with three places and back rests on which were carved in large letters the name of the railroad. On this bench he could lie down and rest a little at night, but seldom did so, because there was always too much work to be done. There were also two roughhewn chairs. Between the windows hung a colored portrait of Kaganovitch in a railroad official's uniform. A huge map of the railroad used to hang there, but the Captain, the Commandant of the station, ordered it taken down because many people came into this room and if there should be an enemy agent among them, he could easily orient himself and discover which railroad went where.

"I got some stockings," Aunt Frosia was boasting in the next room. "A pair of silk stockings for five potato cakes! There may not be any more stockings from now till the end of the war. Tell your mother that she shouldn't lose the opportunity. She should make something out of her potatoes, and go there to the converted car with them. How they snatch them out of your hands! Grunka Mostrukova came back with some kind of a strange night-gown — a woman's — for nighttime — really! — with cut-outs — listen! — in such places! Really it's so funny! The women gathered in her *izba* [peasant hut] to watch her try it on. They laughed so hard they got a stomach-ache! You can also get soap from them — and cheap! Soap is now a defective product — you can't buy it. Tell your mother not to let this pass by!"

"I don't know, Aunt Frosia . . ."

"What? You don't need stockings?"

"I need stockings very much, but somehow it seems a shame — taking from those evacuees!"

"You mean you should take from those who were uprooted! They carry bolts of cloth — they've got suits — they've got soap — enough of everything. They are dressed up as if they were at a country fair! What ugly faces these travelers have! Give them boiled chicken, you hear me?! They don't want anything else! I've even heard that some of them have hundred ruble notes tied in packs, and suitcases full of 'em! Do you think they robbed a bank? But we don't need money — they can take that with them!"

"But what about the people quartered at your place?"

"Don't compare them with the others! They're poor, even barefoot. They ran from Kiev with only what they had on. How they ever reached us is a miracle. Pauline is working at the post office but her salary is very little, and besides, what good is her salary? I took the old woman over and opened up the cellar. 'Here,' I said, 'take yourself some potatoes and sauerkraut, and as for the room, I won't take anything!' I'm sorry for the poor people, Valya, but as for the rich, just don't let 'em ask for mercy!"

On Zotov's desk were two telephones. One was for the railroad, an antiquated crank-type in an old yellow box, the same as the dispatcher's. The other was his own, a buzzer, army field-type, which was connected with the Captain's office and with the guardroom of the station's ration distributing point. The soldiers at the distributing point were the only military troops in the Krechetovka command. Although their main purpose was to guard the food-stuffs and supplies, they also cleaned and heated the place and right now in front of the stove stood an extra bucket full of large glistening lumps of coal to be used at will.

The railroad telephone rang. The sad and lonely feeling immediately passed as Zotov ran quickly to the phone and reached for the speaking tube with one hand while with the other he put his cap back on his head. He began to shout into the phone. He always shouted on long distance calls, sometimes because the connections were bad, but mostly because he was used to speaking loudly.

The call was from Bogoyavlensk and they wanted to verify which routings he had received and which he had not. The routings had been sent by telegraph along with coded instructions from the previous command about which transports were moving and in what direction. Only an hour ago Zotov himself had sent off several such telegrams and got some back. From the messages received he had to find out quickly which transports to put into what groups and stations, which cars to hook up together, and then give the instructions to the railroad Army dispatcher. He also had to prepare and send off new directions, filing one copy for himself.

Putting down the telephone, Zotov sat down quickly, leaned nearsightedly over his desk, and began to dig deep among his routing papers.

Again the two women in the other room disturbed him. A man, stamping his feet loudly, entered and threw a leather satchel full of iron tools on the floor. Aunt Frosia asked about the rain — was it letting up? The man growled out something and apparently sat down.

(It was true that, through the damaged drainpipe, the rain was not as loud as it had been, but the wind was getting stronger and shook the window panes.)

"What did you say, old man?" he heard Valya Podshebyakina ask.

"I said it's getting colder," the old man answered in a deep voice.

"Can you hear, Gavrila Nikitich?" asked Aunt Frosia in a loud voice.

"I hear," said the old man. "There's just a little crackling in my ears."

"Then how do you verify whether the cars are empty or full, grandfather? You know you have to tap on them, like a melon."

"I can also tell by looking at them."

"You may not know it, Valya, but he's a native son; he's from Kordubailo. The wagon masters of many stations are all his trainees! For ten years before the war he lolled on top of the stove. And now, you see, he's out of retirement!"

Again and again Aunt Frosia began talking about something or other and Zotov was getting tired of all this chatter. But he really wanted to get up and scare her away when she began to talk about the incident which had taken place yesterday with the echelon of stragglers.

Zotov had learned about this incident from his alternate on the other shift, who was also an aide to the Army Commander. His alternate had had to take over yesterday because the regular Krechetovka staff Commander was absent from the station. Yesterday morning two transport echelons had arrived together. One echelon which came from Stchiger through Otrozhka was carrying thirty carloads of stragglers, and for these thirty carloads of desperate people there were only five NKDV escorts, who naturally couldn't do anything with them. The other echelon, from Rtistchev, was loaded with flour. The flour was carried partly in lead-sealed cars, partly in half-cars, in sacks. The stragglers immediately grasped the situation, and attacked the half-cars. They climbed to the top, cut open the flour sacks, and filled their mess kits. They turned their jackets into makeshift satchels and filled them too. With the convoy, which accompanied the flour echelon, came two guards, one at the head of the train and the other at the rear. The guard at the head of the train, who was still quite a young boy, yelled at the stragglers a few times to stop taking the flour, but nobody paid any attention to him, and no one came to help him from the "converted" convoy car. Then he raised his rifle, fired, and with a single shot, killed

11

one of the stragglers on top of the half-car on the spot.

Zotov listened and listened to the women's conversation; it was supposed to be thus and so. He couldn't stand it any longer; he had to go in to explain how it really was. Opening the door, he looked at the three of them through his plain round glasses.

On the right side of the table sat the slender Valya, working over the lists and graphs, putting them into different colored boxes.

Along the window, which was covered with a blue masking-paper blind, was a simple wooden bench on which Aunt Frosia was sitting. She was no longer young, had a tough look and the competent, masculine build which is usual with Russian women who are accustomed to hard work either on the job or at home. The wet, gray-green tarpaulin coat which she wore when on duty was twisting out of shape on the wall. She was sitting, her wet boots on, in a black, worn-out civilian topcoat, and was trying to fix the wick which she had taken out of her handy, four-cornered lantern.

At the entrance was pasted a pink paper sign (they were pasted all over Krechetovka) which read: "Beware of Typhus." The pink pieces of paper were like a disease itself, like a rash, on the scorched iron skeletons of the bombed cars.

The old man sat down flat on the floor not far from the door so as not to leave any footprints, a little to the right of the stove, and leaned back against the wall. Beside him lay his old leather satchel with heavy tools, pushed aside lest it be in somebody's way. He was wearing dirty, greasy gloves. He had not bothered to shake off any of the rain, and his boots and raincoat made little puddles of water on the floor where he was sitting. An unlighted lantern, the same kind that Aunt Frosia had, stood between his legs, which were bent at the knees. Under his raincoat, the old man had on a black, wrinkled, long, heavy tunic which was tied at the waist with a dirty gray belt. His hood was untied and thrown back in folds. On his head, which still had curly hair, was a tight-fitting and very old rail-road cap with a visor. The visor shaded his eyes from the light, but the tip of his red nose could be seen, as well as his thick lips, with which he was then wetting a cigarette he had rolled up, using news-paper. He began to smoke. His shaggy, bushy beard was mixed with gray, but still was very black.

12

"What happened to him?" asked Valya, tapping her pencil. "You know, he was at his post — he was the watchman."

"Yeah, that's right," nodded the old man, letting the red ash from his cigarette fall on the top of his lantern and on the floor. "That's right. Everyone wants to eat . . ."

"Why did you say that?" frowned the girl. "Who is . . . 'everyone?' "

"It might even include you and me," sighed Kordubailo.

"Oh, you're an incoherent old man! Why should the stragglers be hungry? They get their food rations from the State. Do you think they'd travel without their food rations?"

"Well, yes, you're right," agreed the old man, and some ashes fell from the cigarette again, this time on his knee and his tunic.

"Watch out . . . You'll burn, Gavrila Nikitich!" warned Aunt Frosia.

The old man watched calmly, without making a move, as the red tobacco ash turned gray on his dark, wet, padded trousers, and when it was completely out, he slowly raised his gray, shaggy head in the visored cap.

"Have you gals ever eaten uncooked flour mixed with water?"

"Why uncooked?" asked Aunt Frosia, in surprise. "Mix it, knead it, and pop it in the oven!"

The old man smacked his pale, thick, lips and did not reply at once. When he did speak, the words did not come out all at once but seemed to limp out slowly as if they were on crutches, "It is obvious, my dear ones, that you have never known hunger."

Lieutenant Zotov came into the room and interrupted the conversation, "Listen, old man, do you know what an oath means? You can imagine, can't you?" (Zotov accented the vowels heavily.)

The old man looked at the young lieutenant dully. Kordubailo was not a big man, but his boots were large and heavy, filled with water and, in places, covered with thick clay.

"What else?" he grumbled. "I have already taken an oath five times."

"And on whose name did you swear? Czar Mikolashka?" [Derogatory for Nicholas.]

The old man shook his head, "Go back farther . . ."

13

"Well, then Alexander III?"

The old man sadly smacked his lips, continued smoking and said, "Right! And now they swear in the name of 'the people!' Is there any difference?"

The cigarette ashes again fell on his knee.

Valya interrupted angrily, shaking the fallen curls back from her face, "Whose flour is it? Doesn't it belong to the people? Whom were they carrying the flour for? For the Germans?"

"Well, you're right." The old man didn't argue. "But the stragglers, the young men who fled were not Germans; they were our people."

He finished smoking the newspaper cigarette to the end, then crushed it out on the top of the lantern.

Zotov was touched, "The old man is mistaken. Do you understand a government order? If everyone takes whatever he wants, if I take — you take — Can we possibly win the war that way?"

"And why did they cut up all the flour sacks?" retorted Valya, fuming. "How does that help? Are these our people?"

"Perhaps because they were sewed up," Kordubailo replied, wiping his nose with his hand.

Aunt Frosia was disturbed, "But why quarrel? Because it was all scattered? Along the tracks? How many did they cut up? How much did they pour out, Comrade Lieutenant? How many children could have been fed with it?"

"True — true," said the old man. "And in this rain, what's left in the gondolas will get soaked!"

Zotov thought to himself: "What can you say to him?" and he became more and more annoyed with himself for getting involved in this useless and befuddled conversation. He said aloud to the others, "Don't make so much noise here! You're disturbing my work."

Aunt Frosia finished cleaning the wick, lit it, and pushed it back into the lantern. She stood up and reached for her stiff, wrinkled raincoat.

"Well then, Valya, sharpen me a pencil and I'll go copy the numbers from 765."

Zotov went back to his own room.

Yesterday's story could have had a worse ending. The stragglers,

14

when they saw that one of their friends had been killed, left the flour sacks, and with a loud roar threw themselves on the young watchman. They had snatched his rifle away from him — it seems he even gave it up without any resistance — and had begun to beat him, and would have literally torn him to pieces if, at last, the corporal of the guard hadn't arrived in time. He saw the situation, arrested the young watchman, and took him away.

When there are stragglers on the trains, every command tries to get rid of them as fast as it can. Last night there was another such echelon, No. 245413, from Pavelitz to Archeda. Zotov received it and sent it quickly through. The echelon stayed in Krechetovka about twenty minutes. The stragglers were sleeping and did not come out. When there are a lot of them together, they are bold and dangerous. They are not a part of the Army; they have no weapons; but they think of themselves as yesterday's army. These are the same young boys who in July were somewhere in Bobruisk, who were in Kiev in August, or who were in Orel in September.

Zotov was a little afraid of them — it was the same feeling, probably, that had made the young watchman give up his rifle without any more shooting. Zotov was ashamed of his situation in such an administrative post as this. He envied the stragglers and was even ready to assume some of their faults, if only he could know that right behind him were the fighting, shooting, and the line crossings!

All of Zotov's classmates and friends were at the front.

And he was stuck — here!

All the more reason to work persistently! To work hard, not only to keep things up-to-date on the shift, but also to have time to do other things! He had to work to the best of his ability and strength during these days, because this autumn was the twenty-fourth anniversary of the Revolution. It used to be the favorite holiday of the year, a happy one regardless of the weather, but this year the very thought of it tore him up inside!

Besides all his daily duties, a special incident had weighed heavily on Zotov for the past week. The event took place during his shift. There had been an air raid on the station, and the Germans had pretty well bombed out the train with the Army cargo in which there were also foodstuffs. If they had only wiped it out completely, the affair would have ended right there. But, fortunately, much of the cargo remained. So Zotov was required to prepare a full report in quadruplicate of everything not destroyed: how much of the cargo was useless and how much could be salvaged? These items had to be classified according to their usefulness and/or replaced by new issue. For example, goods which were from forty per cent to eighty per cent damaged would require a special decision as to their disposition. Cargo which was from ten per cent to forty per cent damaged would be sent on to its destination and exchanged there for new. Finally, there was the cargo which was completely undamaged. To complicate matters, all the goods couldn't be stored in the warehouses at one time. Since many people who were not employed there kept walking through the station, it was easy to suspect them of taking whatever they could. Besides this, in order to determine the percentage of usefulness satisfactorily, it was necessary to call in experts. They came from Michurinsk and from Voronezh and, because they couldn't get any helpers, took a long time going through the boxes in the warehouses.

Even an idiot can drop bombs, but try and put things back in order again!

However, Zotov himself was very orderly and punctual in everything he did, and for this reason had made great progress on these lists. He would work hard on them today, and within a week, finish everything.

In addition to all that, he also had his daily tasks to keep up with. But Zotov also saw himself in perspective to such work. Here he was, a well-educated man with an orderly and systematic mind, doing administrative work, and getting good experience. He could see clearly now all the things that had been wrong with the mobilization orders when the war overtook them, and the deficiencies in Army supply organization. But he could also see many obvious improvements which could have been effected in military administrative work. Was it not his duty to observe, note, correct, then forward his reports to the Peoples' Commissariat of Defense? Even if his efforts could not be utilized in this war, they could be taken into account in the next!

So, for any kind of work, you only had to find the time and

energy (although if you said so to the Captain or to the rail junction Commander — shortsighted people — they would laugh at you!)

He had to make out routing lists as quickly as possible! Zotov rubbed his short, stubby fingers together, took an indelible pencil and, matching the codes, transcribed to several other lists the numbers of the cargo and its respective cars. Sometimes the numbers were small, sometimes they were several digits long. He wrote in a clear, round hand, since there could be no errors in this work. It must be as accurate as gunfire aimed at a target.

He put himself completely into his work, with his brow slightly wrinkled and his lower lip protruding.

There was a light knock on the glass door, and Podshebyakina opened it, "May I come in, Vasili Vasilitch?"

Without waiting for an answer she entered, carrying a list in her hands.

Generally, she was not supposed to enter here. It was possible to settle a question at the threshold of the door or from her room. But he never had any disagreement with her while on duty, and was simply too polite to forbid her to enter. Accordingly, he turned his cipher over and, as though accidentally, covered the column of figures he was writing with a clean sheet of paper.

"Vasili Vasilitch, I have a complication, here, look . . ."

There was no second chair nearby, so the girl leaned over the edge of the table, turning her list, with its uneven row of small figures, toward Zotov. "Here in echelon 446 is car number 57831. Where is it supposed to go?"

"I'll tell you right away." He opened his desk drawer, decided which of three file fasteners to pull out, and opened it (but in such a way that she couldn't see), and found what he wanted, "57831 goes to Pachelma."

"Aha!" said Valya. She wrote *Pach* but made no motion to leave.

With the pencil to her lips, she continued to look at her list, still leaning over the desk.

"You didn't write the name of the town right," Zotov corrected her. "You'll read it wrong, and it will go to the wrong town."

"Really," Valya responded quietly. "Let it go, Vasili Vasilitch.

17

Don't quibble with me." She looked at him through a stray blond ringlet, but she corrected the spelling.

"Then, there's something else . . ." she continued, and again put the pencil to her lips. Her thick flaxen curls fell down over her forehead and covered her eyes, but she didn't push them back. They were so clean and they looked so soft! Zotov imagined how nice it would be to tousle them with his hands! "Now what — platform 105110?"

"Is it a small platform?"

"No, a large one."

"I doubt it."

"Why?"

"One digit is lost."

"What shall I do now?" She threw back her hair. Her eyelashes were almost as blond as her hair.

"Look for it, what else? You must pay closer attention, Valya. Is it the same echelon?"

"Uh-huh."

Looking through the file fastener again, Zotov began to search for the number.

Valya looked at the lieutenant, at his funny ears which stood out from his head, at his nose which was like a potato. His eyes, which she could see clearly through his glasses, were pale blue, with flecks of gray. At work he was stern and strict, but he wasn't bad, this Vasili Vasilitch! What she especially liked in him was that he was quiet and well-mannered.

"Eh!" Zotov became angry. "I should give you a thrashing! It's not one zero five but two zeros five, you blockhead!"

"Two-o-o zeros!" Surprised, she wrote in another zero.

"You finished ten years of school, aren't you ashamed?"

"Oh, stop it, Vasili Vasilitch, what does my ten years of school have to do with it? And where's it supposed to go?"

"To Kirsanov."

"Da," Valya wrote it down.

But she didn't leave. Still leaning over in the same position, not too far from him, she became lost in thought, and with one finger began to play with a splintered piece of wood on the desk.

The young man's eyes involuntarily looked at her young, girlish breasts which were clearly outlined now, but which were usually hidden under the heavy railroad jacket.

"Soon our working day will be over," Valya pursed her lips which were young, fresh, and rosy-pink.

"Until it ends there's still a lot to do!" frowned Zotov, as he looked away from the girl's body.

"You're going back to the old woman's house, aren't you?"

"Where else can I go?"

"Don't you ever visit anyone?"

"As if I had time for visiting!"

"What's there so good at the old lady's? You don't even have a good bed. You sleep on an old chest."

"How do you know that?"

"Everyone knows it and they talk about it."

"This is no time to be sleeping on anything soft, Valya. Especially for me. I'm so ashamed that I am not at the front!"

"Why? Aren't you working hard? What's there to be ashamed of? Don't worry, the time will come for you to be in the trenches, if you're still alive. But until then we should, we must, live like human beings."

Zotov took off his cap which had irritated his forehead. (It was too small for him but he couldn't find another one at the supply depot.)

Valya was doodling idly with her pencil on the corner of her list.

"Why did you leave Avdaev's house? It was much better for you there."

Zotov dropped his eyes and blushed deeply. "I just left — that's all!" (Is it possible that everyone also knew about his difficulty at Mrs. Avdaev's?)

Valya continued with her doodling.

Both were silent.

Valya squinted at his round head. Without the glasses the head would look rather childish with its locks of thin, light hair that seemed to form question marks.

"You don't ever go to the movies. You probably have many interesting books. Maybe you could let me read some."

Zotov straightened himself. The color did not leave his face.

19

"How did you know about the books?"

"I just thought so."

"I don't have any books with me. I left them at home."

"You just don't want to lend them."

"No. I say I don't have any. Where would I carry them? A soldier can take only his duffel bag — nothing else is allowed."

"Then borrow some from us to read."

"Do you have many?"

"Yes. There's a shelf full."

"What kind?"

"*The Blast Furnace, Silver Prince,* and others."

"Have you read them all?"

"A few of them." Suddenly she raised her head, looked at him clearly, sighed, and exclaimed, "Vasili Vasilitch! Come and live with us! Vovka's room is empty, and it will be yours. The stove is nearby and keeps it warm. Mother will cook for you. What makes you stay at the old woman's place?"

They looked at each other — each puzzling over his own thoughts.

Valya saw that the lieutenant was wavering, that he would soon agree. And why shouldn't he agree, this strange man? All the other soldiers always say that they aren't married. He's the only one who admits that he is. All the soldiers were quartered with good families in the village, with warm rooms and good care. Valya wanted a man to live in the house which her father and brother had left to go to war. After their work was done in the late evening, along the darkening and muddy roads of the village, they could go home together (and it would be necessary to hold his hand!), and then they could sit together happily at dinner, tell jokes, and just talk to each other . . .

But Vasya Zotov was almost afraid to look at this girl who openly invited him to her house. She was only three years younger than he and when she addressed him by his patronym, and said "Sir," it was not because of the age difference, but out of respect for his rank as a lieutenant. He knew it would not end with a tasty supper made from his dry rations and with the warmth of the stove. He was becoming excited. Soon he would want to hold her in his arms and stroke her unruly, blond, curly hair.

But — this was impossible.

Although it wasn't really bothering him, he straightened his collar with the red square on the green tab, and adjusted his glasses.

"No, Valya, I won't go anywhere else. However, our work is waiting for us. What are we sitting here talking for?"

He put his cap back on his head, whereupon the expression on his open, snub-nosed face became very stern.

The girl looked at him sullenly and agreed, "Well, all right, Vasili Vasilitch!"

She sighed. With great difficulty she raised herself from her leaning position and, holding the list in her hand, went out.

He blinked, confused and perplexed. Maybe, if she would come back and ask him once more, firmly, he would agree.

But she didn't come back.

Zotov couldn't explain to anyone why he lived in the poorly heated, grimy *izba* with the old woman and her three grandchildren, and slept on the short, hard, uncomfortable chest. The enormous, cruel mob in the barracks where he lived in 1941 laughed at him on the few occasions when he said that he loved his wife and would remain true to her during the entire war, and that he had complete confidence in her, too. His practical-minded friends all laughed wildly, patted him on the shoulder, and advised him not to waste himself. Since then, he had never spoken to anyone about this, but he was very lonely, especially when he woke up in the dark of the night, and thought about his wife, and about how things were for her there, far, far, away, awaiting the birth of his child, and under the German occupation.

But it was not because of his wife that he refused Valya; it was because of Pauline.

Not only because of Pauline, either, but because of . . . he really didn't know.

Pauline, a dark, short-haired woman from Kiev, with a dull, lusterless face, was the one who lived with Aunt Frosia and worked at the post office. Whenever he had time, Vasili would go to the post office and read the latest newspapers (the bundles were always a few days late). He would frequently read the news in all the papers, not in just one or two. Certainly the post office was not a library and nobody was obliged to allow him to read, but Pauline understood how he felt and always brought the newspapers to the end of the counter where he stood in the cold and read. As with Zotov, so also with Pauline, the war was not an insensate swing of an ever-moving wheel; rather it touched the vital center of her life now and for all future time. In order to guess what the future might hold, Pauline would open the newspaper anxiously and with trembling hands and would search for bits of news that would tell her how the war was progressing. They often read together and showed each other the most important places in the news. For both of them these newspapers replaced the letters which neither ever received. Pauline read carefully through all the reports of military episodes, trying to guess if her husband had been involved. On advice from Zotov she even read the articles about machine-gun and tank tactics in *Red Star* [the Army newspaper], wrinkling her smooth forehead over them. Vasili read aloud to her, excitedly, articles by Ilya Ehrenberg. Sometimes he asked Pauline if he could clip some articles for himself from papers that were not delivered.

He fell in love with Pauline, her child, and her mother, in a way that people who have never known misfortune cannot understand. He always brought some sugar from his own rations for her little son. During all the times that they read the newspapers together, he never once dared touch her pale hands, not because of her husband nor because of his wife, but because of the sacred grief that united them.

Pauline was the person closest to him in Krechetovka — no, on this side of the entire front! She represented the eyes of his conscience and his truth. How could he go to live with Valya? What would Pauline think of him?

Even without Pauline, he could not have casually consoled himself with any woman when everything he loved was in danger of being lost.

It was also not easy to admit to Valya and to the lieutenants on the shift that there were evenings when he read a particular book, the only one which he had taken from some library during his bustling travels that year, and which he always carried with him in his duffel bag.

The book was the thick, blue first volume of Karl Marx's *Capital,* printed on the rough paper of the 1930's, which had turned dark with age.

During all the five years of his student days, he had dreamed of reading this most desirable book. More than once he got it out of the Institute library and had tried to make a synopsis of it. He kept the book out by the semester — by the year — but there was never any time. There were always meetings to attend, social burdens, and examinations. Without having finished a single page of his summary he returned the book, at the time of the June examinations. Even when they were studying political economy, the best time to read *Capital,* the teacher talked him out of it, saying, "You'll drown in it." Instead he advised him to use Lapidus as a textbook and to take notes from the lectures. Really, there was not time for anything else.

Now in the autumn of 1941, in the glow of great anxiety, Zotov could find time here in this hole for *Capital.* So he did, when off duty in hours spared from his general education or from District Party Committee tasks. In his quarters at Avdaev's house, in the living room which was filled with philodendron and aloe, he sat at a rickety little table. He read by the light of a kerosene lamp (a small diesel engine wasn't adequate to provide power for all the houses in the settlement), stroking the rough pages with his fingers. He read it, the first time for comprehension, the second for marking and underscoring, and the third for a rapid summary, trying finally to get it all through his head. The worse the news from the war became, the more he buried himself in this thick, blue book. Vasili thought that if he could assimilate everything in just this one volume and memorize all of it in an orderly fashion, he would be invincible, invulnerable, and could not be overcome in any ideological skirmish.

But there were few such hours and few such evenings; he made notes on only a few pages because Antonia Ivanova got in the way.

She, too, was living at Avdaev's house, having come from Lysok, and remaining there in Krechetovka. She soon became the manager of a dining room. She was very enterprising, and such a buxom and strong woman that there wasn't much scandal connected with her dining room. As Zotov later found out, in exchange for one ruble she covered the bottom of a clay bowl with hot, gray, greaseless water in which a few noodles were swimming. For a deposit of another ruble, those who didn't want to drink all this out of the bowl could use a cracked wooden spoon. For herself, Antonia Ivanova would tell Avdaev to set up the samovar, and then would bring bread and fresh butter to her hostess' table. She couldn't have been more than twenty-five years old, but had the appearance of a mature woman with her blond hair combed straight back from her face. She always greeted the lieutenant warmly and cordially; he answered her absent-mindedly, and for a long time thought she was a near relative of the owner of the house. Leaning over his volume he didn't hear her returning late from work, and didn't notice that she kept walking through his living room which gave access to her own bedroom, from there to the owner's room and back again to her own.

Suddenly, she came up to him and asked, "What are you always reading, Comrade Lieutenant?"

He covered the volume with his notebook, and answered her, reluctantly.

On another occasion she asked, "What do you think, isn't it dangerous for me to leave my door unlocked at night?"

Zotov answered her, "What's there to be afraid of? I'm here — with my pistol!"

Again, a few days later, sitting over his book, he realized that the walking back and forth had ceased as if she had left her room. He looked up and was dumbfounded! Right there in his room she had fixed herself a place to sleep on the divan, and was already lying down, with her hair falling over the pillow and her bare, white shoulders uncovered. He stared at her and didn't quite know what to do.

"I'm not disturbing you here, am I?" she asked, with a little laugh.

Vasili got up, at his wits' end. He had already started to walk rapidly toward her, but stopped at the sight of her fat, thievish face. It revolted him!

He couldn't speak. His throat tightened with revulsion. He turned, closed the volume of *Capital,* found the time and strength to put it back in his duffel bag, and rushed over to get his cap and coat which were hanging on a nail. On the way he took off his belt which was cumbersome with his pistol on it and, carrying it in his hand, dashed out the door without a backward glance.

He went out into the pitch-black darkness. Not even a glimmer of light could be seen — neither from the masking paper-covered windows nor from the darkly overcast sky; and the cold, wet autumn wind still whipped and lashed as it had all day. Stumbling through puddles, holes, and mud, Vasili turned into a side entrance of the station, not realizing at first that he was still carrying his belt and pistol. He seethed with such helpless resentment that he almost wept, as if carried away by the dark stream of his emotions.

After that, life became almost unbearable at Avdaev's. To be sure, Antonia Ivanova no longer greeted him, but she began to take to her room a certain fat-jowled dog, a civilian who wore army boots and jacket as was usual among the civilians during these times. Zotov tried hard to study. She purposely did not close her door so he couldn't help overhearing their jokes and how she squealed and moaned.

That was when he moved to the house of the half-deaf old woman, where he found only a short, hard chest to sleep on.

It didn't take long for the gossip to get around Krechetovka. Had it reached Pauline yet? That would be embarrassing.

He had been distracted from his work by these thoughts. He picked up the indelible pencil and forced himself deep into the matter of rail routings. When he had established new routings, he transcribed the numbers of the transports and their consignments to his list in duplicate in his firm, round hand. He would have finished his work, but there was some question about how to divide up a large transport from Kamishin. Only the Commandant himself could decide the question as to how it should be broken down. Zotov picked up the receiver, cranked the telephone, and waited. He gave a longer crank and then another long one. The Captain didn't answer. Obviously, he wasn't in his office. Perhaps he had gone home after supper. But he would have to return to hear the reports before the duty officer for the next shift arrived.

Behind the door, Podshebyakina was talking over the tele-

25

phone to the station dispatcher. Aunt Frosia had come and gone.

Then he heard the heavy footsteps of four boots. They stopped at the door, someone half opened it, and a clear, loud voice asked, "May we come in?"

Without waiting for an answer, they entered. The first one, a lithe young man with a pink, cold, face and the build of a grenadier, stepped into the center of the room, saluted, clicked his heels, and reported: "The commander of convoy transport 95505, Sergeant Gaidukov. Thirty-eight pullman cars, all in order, all ready to move on."

He was dressed in a new winter cap, and a long, well-formed Commander-type coat cut to his measure. Around his waist was a broad leather belt with a star-buckle. His boots were dry and polished.

Behind him, a second, thickset man with a dark, swarthy face eased forward slightly, remaining close to the door. He half-reluctantly raised five fingers to his field cap, modeled after Marshal Budenny's helmet, with its fur-trimmed unbuttoned ear flaps. Without reporting, he said, "The leader of convoy transport 71628, Sergeant Digen. Four sixteen-ton cars."

His enlisted man's overcoat was clasped with a narrow canvas belt. One skirt of it was all twisted or chewed up, as if by a machine; his tarpaulin boots, which were pleated like an accordion, were worn and split. Sergeant Digen's countenance had the eyebrows and jaws of Tchkalov's face [a Russian aviator hero]. However, it was not the face of the brave young Tchkalov who had recently been killed, but what his countenance would have looked like as a tired, old man.

"Well! I'm very glad, very glad," said Zotov, getting up.

Neither by his rank, nor by the nature of his work, was he required to stand and greet every sergeant who entered. But he was sincerely glad to see each of them, and always tried to do everything he could to make their work easier. He had no subordinates assigned directly to him, and these men, whether they came for five minutes or for two days, were the only ones before whom Zotov could display a commander's concern and posture.

"I know, I know your cargo has already arrived," he said as he

26

went to the desk and looked them over. "Here they are, 95505, 71628." He raised his friendly eyes to the sergeants.

Their caps and coats were only slightly wet, with a few large drops of water clinging here and there.

"Why, you're almost dry! Has the rain stopped?"

"Only intermittently." Gaidukov shook his head, smiling, standing not as if at attention, but in a relaxed way. "But the north wind is blowing stronger."

He was only about nineteen but his features had the maturity and confidence that comes from having served in the front lines, like a sun tan from the sun. (It was this air of front-line maturity that caused Zotov to get up from his table.)

Zotov had few helpers at this station. In most cases, it would do no good to confide to those he had the nature of their cargo, because they could go to the cars, and he would have no way of knowing what they might carry off. But men like these! The commandant of a routing station needed more men like them! They impressed him, the one with his cheerful face, the other with his gloomy look.

Gaidukov wanted to know if the Commandant, whom he did not regard as a rear-echelon rat, didn't want to go out and examine his echelon and cargo at once. Not that he was afraid of anything concerning his cargo. He not only took good care of it, but he loved it. It consisted of several hundred beautiful horses, and the quartermaster had loaded the echelon with plenty of hay and oats, not expecting any could be had along the route. Gaidukov had grown up on a farm and had been with horses from childhood. He walked among them now as among old friends. It was more of a pleasure than a duty for him to take care of them, and he always helped the soldiers on duty to water, feed, and look after them. He would open the door and climb up a hanging wire ladder into the car, carrying a "flying bat" [a specially made lantern] in his hand. All sixteen horses in the car — brown, red, black, gray — would turn their long, attentive, intelligent faces toward him and look at him with their large, sad, unblinking eyes, moving their keen ears slowly back and forth not only as if they were asking for hay, but also as if they were asking him to tell them where they were going in this big, noisy box, and why. Gaidukov went among them, pushing among their warm bodies covered with shedding hair and, when there were no other soldiers around, he stroked their soft noses and talked to them. It was harder for the horses to go to the front lines than for people. The horses needed the front lines like they needed a fifth leg!

Gaidukov was afraid that the young commandant might look into his "converted" car, but obviously the lieutenant was a good guy and he didn't need to be on his guard. Although the soldiers in his convoy were all young and new troops, Gaidukov himself had already been on the main line of resistance, and had been wounded in July at the Dnieper River. He had spent two months in the hospital, had worked in the supply room there, and now he was returning again to the front. Therefore, he was thoroughly familiar with Army rules and regulations and knew how to get around them.

With the horses there were only twenty young soldiers who had to return to their division after the horses had reached their destination. In a few days all these men in their new uniforms would be in wet and dirty trenches on the line. And they would be lucky if they were in trenches instead of behind little hillocks trying to cover their heads and shoulders from German mortar fire which would be pressing them hard. Last summer, the German heavy mortars had bothered Gaidukov most of all. But now, in these few days, he wanted to live warmly, amicably, happily.

In their large warm car, two cast-iron stoves were constantly burning large lumps of excellent coal which had been obtained from other echelons. Their echelon was always passed through quickly, and they had not been held up anywhere. Once every twenty-four hours they stopped to feed and water the horses, and once in three days they stopped to redeem their ration certificates.

Since their echelon moved quickly, people asked to be taken along with them. Although regulations were strict about allowing civilians to ride with the guards of the echelon, Gaidukov and his helpers were friendly and kind, and could not look at the people as they walked, cold and shivering, up and down the roadbeds along their route. They couldn't take all who asked but they didn't say "No" to many. One, some kind of inspector, was allowed to join them for a litre of homemade vodka; another, a red-haired old man, in exchange for some cider. Some were taken in exchange for a piece of suet, others for whatever they could give, and still others for nothing. Particularly, they lured the young women and girls of whom they never tired. They even helped them up as they took them into their warm car. These women and girls kept on traveling and traveling without knowing why or where. Right now in the noisy warm car, the red-haired old man had been telling them many stories of the first World War and how he almost won the Georgian Cross. One of the girls who was quite untouchable, hooted like an owl and sat close by the stove. The others, who were already quite warm, had removed their coats, jackets, and even their blouses. One of the girls, her face almost as red as her sleeveless undershirt, had agreed to wash a soldier's shirts and was now wringing them with her helper. She would strike at him playfully with the wet clothes if he came too close to her. Two other girls were doing the cooking for the soldiers, giving their dry army rations a home-cooked flavor. Another was sitting and mending whatever had gotten torn. They would change positions, eat a little something, and sit around the fire awhile. They sang songs in the rough atmosphere of the car as the train traveled at full speed.

Afterward, without setting up any regular shifts of those who were to keep watch and those who were to rest (they were all equally tired after watering the horses) they crawled away to sleep a little in berths made of roughhewn boards. Like yesterday's, today's group of young married women had just recently sent their own men off to the war. But the girls, who had less restraint, would lie there clasped in the arms of the young men in the half-light and shadows cast by the lantern. How could anyone not feel sorry for a young soldier traveling with an advanced detachment up to the main line of resistance! These might well be the last days of his life!

The main thing Gaidukov wanted from the station Commandant was to be sent on his way as quickly as possible. He also wanted to get some information about the itinerary. Where should he leave his passengers? As for himself, he wanted to know what sector of the front they were fighting on now? Would he pass by his home on his way there?

"So-o," said the young lieutenant, looking at the travelers. "You haven't been traveling together, have you? Weren't your echelons hooked together just recently?"

"Right, only a few stations ago."

Quickly glancing over the papers, Zotov pursed his lips. "Why did they send you here?" he asked Digen. "Weren't you in Ryazhsk?"

"We were," Digen answered hoarsely.

"Why the hell did they send you through Ryazhsk? Weren't you surprised at such stupidity?"

"Will we go on together now?" Gaidukov asked. (On the way he had found out from Digen the direction in which he was going, but he wanted to verify it.)

"As far as Gryazi."

"And afterward?"

"That's a military secret," Zotov replied, pleasantly accenting his vowels. He turned his head and, looking over his glasses, squinted at the tall sergeant.

"Why should it be? It's through Kastorna, isn't it?" Gaidukov asked, attempting to draw out a reply, and bowing slightly to the lieutenant.

"That remains to be seen." Zotov wanted to sound stern, but his lips were almost smiling, and Gaidukov knew that it would be through Kastorna.

"Are we leaving the first thing this evening?"

"Right. I have no reason to hold you."

"I . . . I . . . can't go," creaked Digen heavily, in an unfriendly tone.

"Why? You — you, yourself — are you ill?"

"The whole convoy can't go!"

"What do you mean? I don't understand. Why can't you go?"

"Because we . . . we're not dogs!!" Digen burst out, and his eyes rolled angrily under the lids.

"What kind of talk is this?" frowned Zotov, suddenly standing very erect. "Look here, you must be more careful, sergeant."

He noticed that one of the green triangles had been sewn on Digen's coat by only one tab, and that the other one had been simply bent and pressed into the middle hole. The unbuttoned ear flaps of his field cap hung down on his chest, like burdocks.

Angry and sullen, Digen stared at the lieutenant. Then in a

hoarse voice he wheezed, "We can't go on because . . . for eleven days . . . we've gone hungry!"

"What!" The lieutenant leaned back so hard his glasses fell off one ear. He caught and readjusted them. "How can this be?"

"It happens . . . quite simply."

"Don't you have any ration certificates?"

"You can't eat paper."

"Then why are you still alive? How is it possible?"

"I just happen to be!"

"Why are you still alive?" The empty, boyish question really angered Digen. And for a while he had thought he might be able to get some help from him at Krechetovka station! "Why are you still alive!" He was not alone. Hunger and bitterness had tightened his jaws, and now, wolflike, he stared wearily at the pale Military Commandant's aide in this clear warm room. Seven days ago they had procured some beets at one of the stations. They had picked out two sacksful from the refuse heap. All that week they boiled beets in their mess kits — boiled and ate them. They had already begun to vomit — their stomachs just couldn't take it.

The night before last, when their echelon was in Alexandro-Nevsk, Digen looked at his emaciated soldier-reservists for a while — they were all older than he, and he was no longer young — made a decision, and got up. The wind was blowing hard under the cars and whistling through the cracks. Somehow, he had to appease his insides, if only for a little while. He disappeared into the darkness. When he returned in about an hour and a half, he flung three large loaves of bread on the sleeping bench.

A soldier, sitting nearby, was dumbfounded, "Look! One of them's white!"

"Really?" Digen glanced indifferently at the loaves — "I hadn't noticed."

But you couldn't tell any of this to the Commandant now.

"Why are you still alive!" For the last ten days the four of them had been traveling across their native land as if they had been crossing a desert. They had a cargo of 20,000 long-handled shovels packed in factory grease. They were supposed to be taking them (Digen knew the destination) from Gorki to Tiflis. But evidently all

31

the other cargoes were more urgent than their damned cargo packed in congealed grease.

The third week began and they hadn't even progressed halfway. The last dispatcher uncoupled four of their cars and abandoned them at the most convenient station. With their ration certificates they had obtained a three days' supply of food at Gorki, and another at Saransk. Since then, they hadn't been able to find a ration point open. However, they could have gone hungry another five days and even this would not have been so hard to bear, if they only knew that afterwards they would be able to get their rations for all fifteen days. But both their souls and stomachs languished because of the iron law of all ration distributing points: no rations could be given for the days that had passed. The past is water over a dam.

"Why didn't they give you some rations?" inquired the lieutenant.

"What about you? Will you give us some?" Digen's jaw moved.

When he had jumped from the car, Digen found out from a soldier he met that there was a ration point at this station. But it was already getting dark, and, according to regulations, it would be useless to go to the window.

Sergeant Gaidukov forgot all about the cheerful bearing which he had been maintaining in the presence of the station Commandant, and turned momentarily toward Digen. He reached out and placed his hand on Digen's shoulder, "Bro-ther! Why didn't you say something to me? We'll get you something right away!"

Digen didn't move under the tap on his shoulder, but kept staring at Zotov like a dead man. As for Sergeant Gaidukov, it made him sick to his stomach to think that such a stupid man was one of his own. For all eleven days they had not asked for food from either civilian or military authorities. They knew that in these times there wasn't a scrap of food to spare. No one thought of entering their converted "warm" car which had come uncoupled and lay neglected. Even their tobacco was all gone. Because the warm cars were split and cracked, they had boarded up three out of four windows and it was dark inside even during the day. Digen's group had already used everything they could for firewood, and so, during long stops lasting from twenty-four to forty-eight hours, they sat around the dark stove, and having boiled the beets in their mess kits, tried them with their knives, and were silent.

Gaidukov snapped quickly to attention with a youthful swagger and asked, "May I have your permission to leave, Comrade Lieutenant?"

"You may go."

He ran out. With his own two hands he would get these soldiers some millet meal and tobacco! They hadn't taken anything from that teary-eyed old woman in return for her passage. Well, let her share with the boys and not be greedy. Another passenger, the inspector, would also have to contribute from his trunk containing food.

Zotov pondered, "It's seven o'clock. Our distributing point is closed."

Digen exclaimed, "They were always closed! They're only open from 10 to 5. In Penza I was waiting my turn in line when I heard someone yell that the echelon was leaving. When we passed through Morshansk it was night. We went through Ryazhsk at night, too."

"Wait, wait a minute!" the lieutenant began, "I won't let this business continue — You'll see!"

He picked up the receiver of the field telephone and gave a long crank.

Nobody answered. He gave a triple crank. No answer.

"Damn it!" He gave it another triple crank. "Is that you, Guskov?"

"It's me, Comrade Lieutenant."

"Why isn't there a soldier on duty at the phone?"

"He went out. I just got some buttermilk. Would you like me to bring you some, Comrade Lieutenant?"

"What nonsense! I don't need any."

He didn't say that because Digen was there. As a matter of principle he never let Guskov bring him anything. In order to keep business relationships on a strictly official plane, he never even drank with him after duty. On the contrary, he had already reported to the Captain that Guskov was getting out of hand.

"Guskov! How about this? A convoy just came in with four people who have been without food for eleven days —"

Guskov whistled. "How absent-minded can you get?"

"No, it just happened that way. We've got to help. Listen, we've got to get in touch with Chichishev and Samorukov and have them issue some food in exchange for their ration certificates."

"Where do you think we can find them? That won't be easy!"

"Where? Why, in their quarters! The mud's so thick you sink in it up to your knees. And it's as dark as . . . the black hole of Calcutta. Chichishev lives nearby."

"But Samorukov lives across the tracks. He won't come, Comrade Lieutenant."

"Chichishev will come."

The bookkeeper, Chichishev, was in military service and in charge of supplies. He had received the rank of sergeant, but there was nothing military about him. He was just an ordinary bookkeeper, no longer young, who did his job well. He could hardly talk without his calculating machine. If someone would ask at five o'clock, "What time of day is it?" he would soon hear five clicks on his abacus by way of an answer. Or if someone would say, "When a man (one click of the abacus) lives all alone, life is difficult. He (click! — click) should get married!"

He worked behind a closed latticed window with only a small opening through which the line of clamoring soldiers had to hand him their ration certificates. Chichishev was very hard. He shouted at the soldiers, pushed away their hands, and tried to close the hinged pane in order (so he said) to keep the papers from blowing away. But if he had to deal directly with a crowd or when line officers entered his cubbyhole, his head would snap up on his little shoulders, he would address them as "Brothers," and stamp their papers at once. He was so anxious and eager to please the authorities that he didn't dare refuse anyone wearing officer's insignia.

Zotov thought to himself, "The distributing point is not under my jurisdiction, but still Chichishev won't turn me down."

"But I tell you Samorukov won't come," Guskov insisted.

Samorukov ranked as a first sergeant, but looked with contempt on all lieutenants. A healthy, well-fed brute, he was only the storekeeper and cashier of the ration point, but regarded himself as holding the equivalent rank of a captain. He would arrive fifteen minutes late with a show of dignity, go up to the safes, examine the seals, open the locks, and roll up the window blinds. He did all this with the look on his unfriendly face of someone doing a favor. Whenever soldiers arrived, either as individuals or as groups from the transport echelons or Army commands, including invalids, no matter how many crowded around the window, cursing and shoving and trying to get closer, Samorukov would calmly roll his sleeves up to the elbows, showing his large, fat, smooth arms which looked like a butcher's, and always make some faultfinding remark as he verified the bookkeeper Chichishev's stamp on the torn and wrinkled ration certificates. He slowly weighed out the rations (most probably short-weighting them!), and never worried whether the men would miss their train or not. He purposely arranged quarters for himself across the tracks so he wouldn't be bothered by anyone during his free hours, and he picked out a landlord with a garden and a cow.

A feeling of revulsion came over Zotov as he thought about Samorukov. He hated people like that. They were like the fascists, and the threat from the one was no less than from the other. He couldn't understand why Stalin hadn't issued a decree to have people like Samorukov executed right here in front of the distributing point in the presence of all the people.

"No, Samorukov won't come," Zotov thought to himself.

He was both angry at Samorukov and somewhat intimidated by him, and would not have decided to bother him had it not been for the four sluggish soldiers who had had nothing to eat, not just three or five days, but for eleven! "I'll tell you what, Guskov. Don't send an enlisted man after him, but you go yourself. Don't tell him about the four hungry soldiers, just say the Captain wants to see him at once, through me, understand? Have him come to me; I'll talk to him."

Guskov was silent.

"What's the matter? Didn't you understand my orders? Say 'Yes, sir,' and get going!"

"Have you asked the Captain about it?"

"What business is that of yours? I'm responsible here! The

Captain's gone out. He's not in right now."

"But," Guskov reasoned, "even the Captain won't order him to do it. There's nothing in the regulations about removing the seals at night and opening up shop for two loaves of bread and three herring. . . ."

And that was the truth.

Guskov continued, "And why such a hurry? Can't they wait until ten o'clock? It's only one more night! Let 'em lie on their stomachs, their hunger will ease up that way."

"Yes, but their echelon is leaving right away. It's such a fast one, it would be a pity to uncouple them, and besides, they're late already. Their cargo is expected — it's needed."

"Well, if the echelon is leaving, then Samorukov can't get here in time. To get there and back in this mud, even with a lantern, would take no less than an hour and a half, maybe two."

Guskov was right again.

Digen stood there with his teeth clenched, his sad, weather-beaten face encircled with the fur-trimmed ear flaps of his field cap, and his eyes glued to the telephone. He understood what was happening at the other end of the line. Perplexed, he shook his head and mumbled, "So today is lost, too . . ."

Zotov sighed, covered the mouthpiece so Guskov couldn't hear, and turned to Digen, "What can I do, man? No rations given out today. Could you go on to Graza with the echelon? It's a good one, and you'll be there by morning."

Digen didn't say so, but he felt that the young lieutenant had not been firm enough.

"I won't go! You can arrest me, but I won't go!"

Someone was rapping on the pane of the door. A heavy-set civilian was standing there wearing a wide, woolen kepi with dark gray flecks in it. With a polite bow, he asked permission to enter.

"Come on in! Come on, come on," shouted Zotov, pressing the button on the telephone. "All right, Guskov, hang up! I'll think it over."

The man behind the door had not understood Zotov, so he opened the door slightly and again asked, "May I come in?"

His voice surprised Zotov. It was a deep, rich, pleasantly restrained voice that didn't swagger. The man was dressed in some kind of long, heavy, reddish coat, not an Army type, with sleeves that were too short for him. On his feet were Red Army boots with loosely wrapped puttees. In one hand he held a small, greasy Red Army duffel bag. With the other hand, he raised his impressive kepi slightly and greeted both men as he entered, "How do you do!"

"How do you do."

The stranger carried himself as if his dress were quite proper rather than the strange assortment of clothing it actually was. "Could you tell me, please," he asked very politely, "who's the Army Commander here?"

"I'm the aide on duty."

"Then, perhaps you're the one I want to see."

He looked around for some place to put his speckled kepi, which was covered with coal dust, and finding none, put it under his arm. With his free hand he began to unbutton his long, reddish coat. It was collarless, or rather the collar had been torn off, but around his bare neck was a warm woolen scarf. Under his unbuttoned coat was an old Red Army summer jacket, faded and stained. He began unbuttoning one of the pockets of his field shirt.

Zotov motioned to the stranger to wait. "I'll tell you what . . ." he turned to the sad and motionless Digen, and continued, "I'll do whatever I can. I can uncouple your cars now. Tomorrow at ten, you'll get your rations."

"Thank you," said Digen, and as he looked at the lieutenant, his eyes filled with tears.

"Don't thank me. It's the best I can do. You have just left a good echelon. I can't say what your next one will be like."

Digen was coming back to life. "Give or take a day, we've been on the move two weeks. I can see that my cargo . . ."

"No-o," Zotov raised a warning finger. "It's not up to us to judge." He glanced at the stranger, then went up to Digen and said, in a forceful but barely audible voice, heavily stressing his vowels, "Whenever you look at your cargo — think! Think, how many lives could have been saved with your shovels? Two divisions! Digging in is the only way to save lives. Shovels — 20,000 of them! That's 20,000 Red Army lives! Right?"

Zotov again looked at the man who had come in. The stranger understood that he was in the way and went over to the wall, turned around, and with his free hand, started to cover each ear in turn, or rather he began rubbing them.

"What's the matter? Were they starting to freeze?" Zotov called out loudly, and laughed.

The stranger turned and smiled, "You know, it's turning frightfully cold. The wind is terrible — and a little wet."

And indeed, the wind was blowing and howling around the corner of the building and rattling the loose pane in the right window, behind the blinds. The water rushing through the damaged pipe was getting louder, too.

The unshaven face of the stranger wore a trusting and sympathetic smile. He did not have a military haircut. His powerful head was covered with soft, fairly short hair, not very thick, and touched with flecks of gray. He resembled neither a soldier nor a civilian.

"Here," he held in his hand a piece of paper which had been filled out. "Here is my . . ."

"In a minute, in a minute . . ." Zotov took the paper from him without looking at it. "Sit down. You can take this chair."

He looked at the man's clownish outfit again, then turned and went to his desk, picked up his cipher and register, locked them in the safe, nodded to Digen and went into the adjoining room, the army dispatcher's office. Podshebyakina was talking on the telephone while Aunt Frosia squatted by the stove, drying herself. Zotov went up to Podshebyakina, and clasped his hand over hers while she was holding the telephone.

"Valusha . . ."

The young girl turned quickly and looked at him playfully, since from the way he clasped and held on to her hand, she thought he was caressing it. But she still finished her conversation, ". . . 1,000 on the next load . . . we have nothing for him, Petrovitch. Send him to Tambovsk."

"Valechka!" Zotov continued, "Send Aunt Frosia over quickly to rewrite the orders, or show her directly how to link these four cars together. This young sergeant will go with them. Have the train dispatcher uncouple the lot, and put them somewhere out of the way until morning."

38

From where she was squatting, Aunt Frosia turned her large, stern face toward the lieutenant, and moved her lips.

"Very well, Vasili Vasilitch," Valya smiled. She hadn't removed her hand from the telephone because his hand was still over hers. "I'll take care of it right away."

"Send the rest of the echelon forward with the first available engine. Do your best!"

"Certainly, Vasili Vasilitch," Valya smiled, happily.

"Well, that's all I can do!" the lieutenant announced to Digen. Aunt Frosia sighed like a bellows, and stood up grunting.

Without a word Digen raised his hand to his cap and held it there. He looked lop-eared under his battered field cap, not at all like a soldier, and the lieutenant asked him, "Have you just been inducted? You were a laborer, I suppose."

"That's right," Digen said, looking firmly but gratefully at the lieutenant.

"Screw on your other triangle." Zotov pointed to his empty collar from which the insignia was missing.

"I can't," Digen replied. "It's broken."

"And your cap — either button the flaps or roll them up — understand?"

"And just where would he roll them?" growled Aunt Frosia, already in her raincoat. "The cloth is no good! Come, laddie!"

"Well, all right, and good luck! There'll be another lieutenant on duty tomorrow. You put the pressure on him to send you on your way!"

Zotov returned to his own room, closing the door behind him. He remembered that four months ago he didn't know how to fix his belt or give a good salute either, and it seemed absurd and funny.

On Zotov's return, the visitor did not fully rise but indicated that he would, if necessary. His duffel bag lay on the floor with his softly speckled kepi on top of it.

"Please remain seated," Zotov said as he sat down at his desk. "Now, what can I do for you?" and he unfolded the piece of paper the man had handed him.

"I — I lost my echelon," the stranger smiled guiltily.

Zotov read the piece of paper. It was a list of stragglers sent through by the Ryazhsk military Commandant. He looked at the stranger, and began to ask him some security control questions, "Your family name?"

"Tveritinov."

"Your given name?"

"Igor Dementevich."

"Are you over fifty?"

"No, I'm forty-nine."

"What was the number of your echelon?"

"I can't remember."

"Didn't they tell you the number?"

"No."

"Then why is it here in your papers? Did you put it here?" (The echelon number was 245413 — the very same one that Zotov had sent through last night!)

"No. I told them in Ryazhsk where the echelon came from and where it was going. The Commander probably guessed it."

"Where did you leave it?"

"In Skopin."

"And how did that happen?"

"If I may speak frankly" (the same guilty smile touched Tveritinov's generous lips), "I went to exchange some clothes . . . to try to get some food somewhere, and the echelon left. During these times, they leave without any signals, or bells, or loud-speaker announcements. They take off so quietly."

"When was this?"

"The day before yesterday."

"And you didn't try to catch up with it?"

"Well, obviously, no. How could I overtake it? It was raining on the railway siding. On the platform cars, you know, the ones with the short ladders, it's terribly drafty; besides, the watchmen will drive you away. They won't allow you in the 'converted' car either because you haven't the right, or because there isn't any room. Once, it was like a miracle — I saw a passenger train. But the conductor, who was standing on the top two steps, you know, forcefully pushed away anyone who tried to grab the handrail. As for freight trains, once they start it's too late to get on and when one of them is standing by without an engine, you never know in which direction it will go. There are no enameled name plates like 'Moscow Mineral Springs' on the trains, and you can't ask anyone anything because they'll think you're a spy. And besides — look at my clothes! For us stragglers it's especially dangerous to ask questions!"

"During wartime, certainly."

"Yes, and it was like that before the war, too."

"Well, I hadn't noticed."

"It was," Tveritinov replied, half closing his eyes. "After 1937 —"

"Oh? What about 1937?" Zotov was surprised. "And what was happening in 1937? The Spanish War?"

"Why no-o," Tveritinov replied with downcast eyes and again a guilty little smile, "—no—."

His soft, gray woolen scarf had come loose and hung awkwardly below his belt.

"Why aren't you in uniform? Where's your overcoat?"

"I didn't get one. They didn't issue us any," smiled Tveritinov.

"Where did you get that outfit?"

"Some helpful people gave it to me."

"M-m, well . . . ," Zotov became thoughtful. "I must say, you got here rather quickly. Yesterday morning you were at headquarters in Ryazhsk and this evening you're here. How did you travel?"

Tveritinov looked at Zotov with his big, soft, and trusting eyes. Zotov liked the brevity of the stranger's replies and the manner in which he conversed, his way of letting the other person speak first, his way of not gesturing with his hands, but somehow, with light movements of his fingers when he spoke.

The stranger continued, "I was especially lucky. At one station I climbed out of a gondola car. After two days I began to decipher railroad terminology. I saw the sign, 'Gondola,' and thought it was supposed to be some sort of car which would at least be covered. I climbed up the ladder and there was simply an iron hole — a trap — with no place to sit down and nothing to lean against. The gondola had formerly carried coal and, as the train moved, a storm of black dust rose up and kept swirling all around. It got all over me. And then it began to rain . . ."

41

Zotov burst out laughing, "So that's what you call 'lucky.' I don't get it. No wonder your clothes are so dirty!" When he laughed, two big, kind laughter lines appeared on each side of his mouth, reaching up to his wide nose.

"That's how. After I got out of the gondola, I shook off some of the dust, washed, and looked around. Then I saw something. They were hitching an engine to an echelon heading south, and I ran alongside it. Well, there wasn't a single warm car attached to the train, and all the doors were sealed. Suddenly I saw a man come out of one of the cars. He relieved himself, and went back into a cold, unsealed, car, and I went in after him! And there inside, just imagine, was a carload of cotton blankets!"

"And the car wasn't sealed?"

"No! You could see that obviously the blankets had been tied in bundles of five or ten, but many of the bundles had come untied and it was very comfortable to bury yourself in them. Several people were already asleep."

"Ay-ay-ay!"

"I covered myself with three or four blankets and slept like a log. A whole twenty-four hours flew by. I don't remember a thing, not even whether we moved or stopped. The third day I didn't even draw my rations, I just slept and slept! I forgot all about the war, all about the stragglers. I even saw my family in my dreams!" His unshaven, unkempt face beamed.

"Stop!" Zotov, suddenly remembered something, and jumped up from his chair, "you were in that echelon? You came with them here? When?"

"Why, only a few minutes ago — I came directly here to you."

Zotov dashed to the door, jerked it open, and shouted, "Valya! Valya! That train going to Balashov, 1,000 and something on your list."

"1,002."

"Is it still here?"

"No. It's gone."

"Are you sure?"

"Positive."

"Oh! Damn it." Zotov grabbed his head. "Here we sit, a

bunch of damned bureaucrats, shuffling our papers, and see nothing. We eat our bread to no purpose. But come on, call Michurinsk-Uralsk quickly!"

He dashed back to his own room and asked Tveritinov, "Don't you remember the number of the car?"

"No," Tveritinov smiled.

"Was it a two-axle or four-axle freight car?"

"I don't understand what you mean."

"Well, why don't you understand? Small or large? How many tons capacity?"

"It was like they used to say during the civil war: 'forty people or eight horses!' "

"That means sixteen tons. Wasn't there any convoy guard?"

"Apparently not."

"Vasili Vasilitch!" shouted Valya. "The military dispatcher is on the phone. Do you want the Commandant?"

"I may and I may not — the cargo may not be military."

"While you're making up your mind, what shall I tell them?"

"Well, you think of something, Valya! Maybe they're just evacuating these blankets, the devil only knows. Tell them to look carefully until they find the car, find out whom it belongs to, and then seal it! And tell them to hurry!"

"Very well, Vasili Vasilitch."

"Please now, Valechka. Now then, you . . . you're a very . . . good worker!"

Valya smiled at him, her curls falling all around her face, "Hello? Michurinsk-Uralsk?"

Zotov closed the door and still excited, walked into his room, rubbing his hands together. "We're swamped with work!" he exclaimed, slightly stressing his vowels. "And they never give us enough help! Why, those blankets could easily be stolen. Maybe they're gone already!"

He walked around for a few more minutes and then sat down. He took off his glasses and began to clean them with a little rag. His face at once began to lose its air of businesslike efficiency and decisiveness and, shaded only by his green service cap, appeared young and boyish.

Tveritinov waited patiently. He looked at the masking-paper blinds, at the colored picture of Kaganovitch in his railroad marshal's uniform, at the stove, and at the bucket with its little shovel. In the warm room his jacket, covered with coal dust, began to bother him. He slipped it off his shoulders, and took off his scarf.

The lieutenant put his glasses back on, and again looked over the straggler list which Tveritinov had handed to him. The list was not an official document since it was based only on the word of the individual applicant who could tell the issuing authority the truth or not. He had strict instructions about carefully questioning and examining stragglers, especially single individuals. Tveritinov couldn't swear that he had left the train in Skopin. Or was it in Pavelitz, perhaps? And between Skopin and Pavelitz, had there been enough time to get to Moscow — or somewhere else — and fulfill a mission? According to his conversation, he certainly reached here fast. On the other hand, what guarantee was there that he actually did come here with this echelon?

"So you had a nice warm journey this time?"

"Certainly! It would have been a pleasure to continue this way."

"Why did you leave the echelon?"

"In order to report to you. They told me to in Ryazhsk."

On Tveritinov's large head all the features were prominent: a wide and high forehead, thick, protruding eyebrows, and a large nose. His chin and jaws were covered with a graying, bristly beard.

"How did you find out that this station was Krechetovka?"

"Someone, a Georgian, who was sleeping next to me — he told me."

"Was he in the service? What was his rank?"

"I don't know. He barely raised his head up from under the blankets," Tveritinov answered a little sadly, as if with every answer he had lost something.

"Well, now," Zotov asked as he put aside the paper, "what other documents do you have?"

"None," Tveritinov answered sadly. "Where would I get other documents?"

"Hmm . . . nothing else?"

"When we were encircled by the enemy, we purposely tore up everything we had."

"But when they received you on Soviet territory, didn't they give you anything to keep with you?"

"Nothing. They made up a list, divided us up into groups of forty people each, and sent us away."

True, it could have been like that. As long as a man remained with his group of forty, he didn't need any documents.

Zotov's naturally favorable inclination toward this man of good manners and education made him want to get just one little something from him that he could examine as material evidence.

"Don't you have anything at all? Aren't there any personal papers of any kind left in your pockets?"

"Only a few photographs of my family."

"Show them to me!" the lieutenant demanded, or rather begged.

Tveritinov's brows raised slightly. He still had that sad little smile on his lips. From the same pocket of his field shirt (the other one wouldn't stay closed since it had no button) he took out a small bundle wrapped in smooth orange-colored paper. He opened it on his knees, and took out two 4 x 5 photographs, gazed at each a moment, and was about to get up and take the pictures over to the Commandant. But from the desk to the chair was only a short distance, and Zotov leaned over, took the pictures, and began looking at them. Tveritinov, continuing to hold the wrapper on his knees, straightened his back and also tried to see from his position.

One picture must have been taken in a small garden on a sunny day, probably in early spring, Zotov thought, because the leaves were still small and curly. Against a background of almost bare trees stood a young girl, about fourteen, in a gray, striped dress with a belt. Her collar was open, and you could see her long, thin neck. Her face was drawn and thin. Although on the photograph it was motionless, yet it suddenly seemed to move, as if startled. The whole picture had an amateurish, unfinished look about it, and achieved a poignant effect which gripped his heart.

Zotov liked the looks of the young girl. His face softened. "What's her name?" he asked quietly.

Tveritinov sat with closed eyes. "Lyalya," he answered, softly. Afterward he opened his eyes and corrected himself, "Irene."

"When was it taken?"

"This year."

"And where?"

"Near Moscow."

Six months! Only six months ago to the day, he had said to her: "Lyalenka! Look here!" as he snapped the shutter.

Since that time, tens of thousands of guns had roared, churning the black earth into millions of fountains, and millions of people had been uprooted and caught in this accursed merry-go-round, some on foot from Lithuania, others by train from Irkutsk. And now in the railroad stations, where the cold wind whipped a mixture of rain and snow, they were waiting for the transport echelons, miserably milling around by day, and sleeping crowded together on the dirty floors at night. How could anyone believe now that in the whole world there had ever existed this garden, this young girl, this dress?

The second snapshot was of a woman and a little boy seated on a sofa looking at a large picture book. The mother was also lean, slender, and rather tall, but the seven-year-old boy had a full, round face, which wore a serious, half-serious expression. He had the same large eyes as his father, and he was looking, not at the book, but at his mother who seemed to be explaining something to him.

There was some kind of a special quality about the whole family. Zotov himself had personally never known such families, but from little cross-recollections of pictures at the Tretyakov Gallery, or of scenes from the theatre, or from his reading, he had gradually come to realize that there were such people. Both pictures reflected a feeling of intelligent warmth and comfort which drifted out over Zotov.

Returning the photographs he observed, "You're warm. Why don't you take off your jacket."

"Yes," agreed Tveritinov, taking it off and looking around for some place to put it.

"There, on the couch," pointed Zotov, making a gesture to take the coat.

Now he could clearly see the torn and patched summer army jacket, with its unmatched buttons and missing pocket. Tveritinov had not done a good job with the puttees, which were loose and droopy. His whole outfit seemed to make a mockery of his large, intelligent head.

46

Zotov couldn't restrain his sympathy for this well-poised man, and for no reason, had at once taken a liking to him.

"And may I ask what you do?" Zotov asked, respectfully.

Sadly replacing the photographs in the orange-paper wrapping, Tveritinov answered, with a little laugh, "I'm an actor."

"Re-ally?" Zotov asked, surprised. "Why didn't I guess at once! You certainly have the appearance of an actor!"

(Right now the stranger couldn't have looked less like one!) ". . . a famous actor probably?"

"No."

"Where did you perform?"

"At the Dramatic Theatre in Moscow."

"I was in Moscow only once at the MXAT [Moscow Art and Academic Theatre]. We were on an excursion. But I used to go to the theatre in Ivanov quite often. Have you seen the new theatre there?"

"No."

"From the outside it looks like a big, gray box made out of reinforced concrete, but the inside is really wonderful! I loved going to the theatre. It's not merely a pleasure but an education. Right?"

(Certainly, the paper work connected with the burnt-out transport echelons and the disposition of the cargo was crying to be done, but even if it took two full days, it was all the same to him. It was wonderful to meet and talk for a while with a great artist!)

"What roles did you play?"

"Many," Tveritinov smiled unhappily. "There were so many years — I can't tell—"

"For instance?"

"Well, I played a Lieutenant Colonel Vershinin, and a Doctor Rank . . ."

"Hm-m-m." (Zotov didn't remember such roles.) "Were you in any Gorky plays?"

"Of course, naturally."

"I like Gorky's plays best of all. Gorky is the greatest! He's our wisest, most human, our greatest writer! Don't you agree?"

Tveritinov sat with knit brows, searching for an answer, but couldn't find one and remained silent.

"It seems that I remember your name. You're sure you're not famous?" Zotov's face was slightly flushed with pleasure from the conversation.

"If I were famous," Tveritinov gestured lightly with his hands, "I probably wouldn't be here now!"

"Why? Oh, I get it, you wouldn't have been mobilized."

"We weren't mobilized. We enlisted. We signed up voluntarily."

"Well, didn't the famous artists also sign up voluntarily?"

"Everybody signed up, from the most important directors on down. Then somebody drew a line: those above the line, stayed, those below, went."

"Did you get any military training?"

"A few days of it — bayonet drills with walking sticks; and how to throw grenades — wooden ones."

Tveritinov's eyes were glued to one spot on the floor so firmly that he looked glassy-eyed.

"And later, did you get weapons?"

"Yes, when we were already on the march, they gave us rifles, Model 901. We walked all the way to Vyazma. Walked right into a pocket."

"Were many killed?"

"I think so, but a great many more were taken prisoners.* A small group of us who had been surrounded joined with other front-line stragglers. They helped us get out. I don't even know where the front is now. Don't you have a map?"

"I don't have a map, and the reports are not clear, but I can tell you this much: Sevastopol is ours, Taganrog is ours, and we're holding our own in the Don basin. But they have Orel and Kursk."

"Oy, oy, oy! . . . And what about Moscow?"

"I especially don't understand about Moscow. Routing directions are all from the suburbs. And Leningrad is completely cut off."

Zotov's eyes and wrinkled brow reflected his sorrow and suffering, "And I can't get to the front!"

"You'll get there yet."

---

* According to captured German records, in mid-October 1941, 685,000 Russian prisoners were taken in the Vyazma-Bryansk encirclements southwest of Moscow.

48

"Yes, but only if the war lasts longer than a year."

"Were you a student?"

"Yes, I had just defended my thesis when the war started. And what a session that was! We had to be ready by December. They told us to bring along whatever we could: drafts, estimates, plans, etc." Zotov spoke almost breathlessly in his eagerness to tell him everything at once. "Why, that was a whole five years ago. We entered the university about the time of Franco's revolution. Then Austria fell — then Czechoslovakia! Then the World War began! Here we had the winter war with Finland! Hitler invaded France! Greece! Yugoslavia! How could we study about textile machines? That wasn't all. After defending their theses, the students were sent for special courses to the motorization and mechanization Academy — I was kept behind because of my eyes. I'm very nearsighted. Every day I stormed into the Military Commissariat. I had had experience dating from 1937, and the only thing I got out of it was that they sent me to the Quartermaster Academy! All right then — with these orders I went to Moscow and threw myself on the Peoples' Commissariat of Defense. I was sent to an old colonel, who was in a terrible hurry to get away. He already had his brief case closed. So I tell him I'm an engineer, that I don't want to work in the Quartermaster Corps. 'Show me your diploma!' he says. I didn't have it with me. 'Well then,' he says, 'I'll give you one question. Answer it, and I'll know whether you're an engineer! What's a crankshaft?' Standing in the doorway, I recited verbatim: 'It's a device which rotates on an axis or universal joint connected to the piston rod which . . .' He crossed out 'Quartermaster' and wrote 'Transportation Academy.' Then he took his portfolio and left. Man, how I celebrated! Then I went to the Academy. There was no recruitment — no beginners — just courses for Army Commanders. My crankshaft didn't help!"

Vasili knew that this wasn't the time to chatter and reminisce, but it was a rare occasion to be able to pour out your soul to such an attentive, intelligent listener.

"You smoke, don't you?" Zotov recollected. "Go ahead and smoke then, please." He glanced at the straggler list. "Here, Igor Dementevich, here's some tobacco and paper. It's issued to me, but I don't smoke."

49

From his drawer he took a package of tobacco which had hardly been used, and pushed it toward Igor Dementevich.

"I do smoke," Igor Dementevich confessed, and his face lit up with anticipated pleasure. He reached for the package of tobacco, but before he took some, he filled his nostrils with the delicious aroma and seemed to moan silently with pleasure. Then he read the label aloud. "It's Armenian," he said, turning his head.

He rolled himself a thick cigarette and sealed it with his tongue.

Vasili lit a match for him, and inquired, "In the car with the cotton blankets, didn't anyone smoke?"

"I didn't notice." Igor Dementevich leaned back blissfully in his chair, "Probably no one had any." His eyes were half-closed. Then he asked Zotov quietly, "And what do *you* remember about 1937?"

"You must remember what happened that summer!" Vasili answered eagerly. "The Spanish war was on! The fascists had taken the university towns. Remember the International Brigade, Guadalajara, Jarama, Teruel? Could we sit idly by? We requested that they teach us Spanish, but no, they taught us German. I got hold of a textbook and a dictionary. I didn't take the tests and examinations, but I learned Spanish anyway. I had a feeling about the whole situation, that we were taking a big part there, and that our revolutionary conscience wouldn't let us sit idly by. But there was none of this in the newspapers. How could I get there? Obviously, the simplest thing would have been to go to Odessa and catch a boat. But this would have been childish, and besides, there was the border patrol. So I went to the heads of the District Military Commissariats in the fourth, the third, the second, and the first districts. 'Send me to Spain!' I said. And they laughed, 'Are you crazy? There are none of us there. What would you do?' . . . You know, I can see how much you enjoy smoking. Take the pack for yourself. I just keep it around for those who smoke. I have some in my quarters, too. No, please put it in your duffel bag; tie it — then I know you'll have it. Tobacco these days is like your 'Passport.' It will be useful on the way. . . . Yes, and suddenly, you remember, I read it in *Red Star* (I read all the newspapers thoroughly) — they quoted a French journalist who among other things wrote: 'Germany and the USSR

50

consider Spain as an experimental proving ground.' So I had been right all along! I went to the library, begged a copy of this issue, and waited three days to be sure the editors wouldn't refute it. They didn't! Then I went to the Military Commissariat and said, 'Here, read this. It hasn't been refuted, therefore it must be a fact that we're fighting there. I beg you to send me to Spain — even as a private! The Commissariat banged on the table. 'You . . . don't you try to provoke me! Who sent you here? If we need you, we'll call you. About face!' "

Zotov laughed heartily as he recalled the incident. The deep laughter lines brightened his face again. He talked without embarrassment to this artist, and wanted to tell him all about the Spanish sailors and his conversation with them in Spanish. He wanted to ask how things were with the stragglers; above all, he wanted to talk with this enlightened and intelligent man about the progress of the war.

But Podshebyakina partly opened the door, "Vasili Vasilitch! The dispatcher wants to know if you have any cars for 794? So we can release it."

Zotov looked at his chart, "Which one is it? To Povorin?"

"Yes."

"It's here already?"

"It'll be here in about ten minutes."

"We have a little cargo. What else is there?"

"Some industrial cargo and several converted passenger cars."

"That's wonderful . . . wonderful! Igor Dementevich, I'll put you on this one! This is a very good train for you; you won't have to get off. No, Valushka, the cargo all goes together. Put it on the passageway. Have them bring it in closer, say, on the first or second track."

"Very well, Vasili Vasilitch."

"Did you tell them about the blankets?"

"I told them about everything, exactly as you said, Vasili Vasilitch." And she left.

"I'm only sorry that I haven't anything to feed you, not even a lump of sugar in my drawer." Zotov opened the desk drawer as if to assure himself that there really wasn't any. His ration was always a small one, and the bread, which was brought when he was on duty, he ate in the morning. "Haven't you had anything to eat since you left the echelon?"

"Don't worry. It's nothing, Vasili Vasilitch." Tveritinov placed a large hand with its fingers spread out like a fan on his dirty field shirt with the unmatched buttons. "I'm already eternally grateful." His look and his voice were no longer sad. "You have warmed me literally and figuratively. You are a good man. In hard times like these, that is especially priceless. And now, please explain to me where I'm going and what else I must do?"

Pleased, Zotov began to explain, "First you will go to the station at Gryaz. I'm sorry I don't have a map. Have you any idea where that is?"

"Not exactly. But I think I've heard the name before."

"It's a very famous station! If you're in Gryaz during the day, take your paper . . . here, I'll mark it to show that you were with me . . . and go to the military Commandant. He'll give you an order to the food distributing point and you'll get rations for a couple of days."

"I'm very grateful to you."

"But if you arrive at night, stay put. Don't get out; just stay with this echelon! You'd have been in trouble with those blankets if you hadn't awakened; they would have arrested you! From Gryaz, your train will go to Povorino, and in Povorino go only to the food point; don't let your train get away! It'll take you as far as Archeda. In Archeda, your echelon will be assigned number 245413."

Zotov gave the paper with the list of stragglers on it to Tveritinov.

As he put it back into the one pocket left in his jacket, Tveritinov asked, "Archeda? That's one I never heard of . . . Where is it?"

"You'll find yourself near Stalingrad."

"Near Stalingrad," Tveritinov nodded. His brow wrinkled. He made an absent-minded effort and asked again, "Permit me . . . Stalingrad . . . What was it called before?"

For Zotov everything came to an abrupt stop and he turned cold! Was it possible? A Soviet citizen who didn't know Stalingrad? No! This couldn't be possible! Never! Never! This was inconceivable!

However, he succeeded in controlling himself, pulled himself together, and adjusted his glasses. When he replied, he spoke almost quietly, "It used to be called Czaritsin."

(So, he's not a straggler. He was sent! An agent! He's probably a White Russian immigrant; that's why he has such beautiful manners.)

"Ah, yes, yes, Czaritsin. The battle of Czaritsin."

(Could he be an officer in disguise? He had asked for a map . . . and had overplayed with his clothes.)

"Officer" was an enemy word which had long since disappeared from Russian speech. Merely to pronounce the word around Zotov was like flashing a bayonet.

(Oh, how gullible! How gullible I've been! So, now remember the motto: *Be calm, Be vigilant!* But what action should be taken?)

Zotov pushed the buzzer on his field telephone. He held the phone to his ear, hoping that the Captain would answer promptly.

The Captain didn't answer.

"Vasili Vasilitch, I feel guilty about taking all your tobacco."

"It's nothing. Please," Zotov objected.

(What a fool I've been to let my guard down! I let the enemy walk over me. I outdid myself trying to please him!)

"Well, then, with your permission, I'll have another cigarette. Or shall I go out to smoke?"

(Him? Go out? It's clear! He's realized his mistake — now he wants to slip away!)

"No. No. Smoke in here. I like the smell of tobacco smoke."

(What can I think of? What's the best way to handle this?)

He pressed the buzzer three times.

Someone picked up the telephone, "Guardroom."

"This is Zotov speaking."

"I'm listening, Comrade Lieutenant."

"Where is Guskov?"

"He . . . went out, Comrade Lieutenant."

"What do you mean he went out? Where to? He's on guard duty! Get him back to his post in five minutes!"

(He probably went out with some wench, the scoundrel!)

"Yes, sir, Comrade Lieutenant, on guard!"

(What can I think of next?)

Zotov took a piece of paper and, holding it in such a way that Tveritinov couldn't see, wrote in large letters: "Valya! Come into my office and say that 794 will be an hour late." He folded the paper, went to the door and from there, extending his hand toward her, said, "Comrade Podshebyakina! Take this. It's about that transport."

"Which transport, Vasili Vasilitch?"

"The number's written here."

Podshebyakina was surprised. She got up and took the paper. Without waiting, Zotov closed the door and turned around.

Tveritinov was already putting on his coat. "We won't miss the train?" he asked with a friendly smile.

"No. They'll call us."

Zotov walked across the room, without looking at Tveritinov. He straightened his field shirt in back under his pistol belt, and transferred the weapon to his right side. He straightened his green forage cap. There was absolutely nothing else to do, and nothing else to talk about.

Zotov didn't know how to lie. He thought to himself, "If only Tveritinov would say something!" But the latter remained modestly silent.

Outside the window, water rumbled through the damaged drainpipe, and was swept and scattered by the wind.

The lieutenant stood by the corner of his desk and examined his fingers.

(In order to keep the stranger from suspecting anything, it was necessary to look at Tveritinov as before — but he couldn't force himself to do so.)

"Well . . . in a few days . . . there will be a holiday!"* he said, with a guarded look.

(That's it! Ask him — ask him: "What *kind* of a holiday?" Then there would be no doubts.)

The guest answered, "Ye-s."

Zotov gave him a quick glance. Tveritinov continued nodding

---

* November 7th, the anniversary of the 1917 Bolshevik Revolution, usually celebrated with a lavish military parade in Moscow.

as he smoked and added, "Very interesting. Will there be a parade in the Red Square?"

(How could there be a parade! He wasn't even thinking about what he was saying, he simply wanted to take up time.)

There was a light knock on the door. "May I come in, Vasili Vasilitch?"

Valya pushed her head in. Tveritinov saw her, and reached for his duffel bag. "Number 794 was delayed on the last stretch. It will be an hour late."

"Oh, no-oo! What a nuisance!" (Even he was struck by the disgusting falseness of voice.) "Thank you, Comrade Podshebyakina."

Valya disappeared.

Through the nearby window could be heard the restrained breathing of an engine becoming slower and lower in pitch as it rolled to a stop and the ground tremors ceased.

"What should I do?" Zotov thought aloud. "I have to go to the distributing point."

"I'll go out, too. I'll go wherever you want me to, certainly," answered Tveritinov willingly, smiling. He was already standing with his duffel bag in his hands.

Zotov took his coat from the nail. "Why go out there and freeze? You can't get into the waiting room because people are sleeping all over the floor. Don't you want to come with me to the ration distributing point?" This sounded unconvincing, and he added, feeling his face turning red, "I . . . maybe I can get . . . can arrange to get you something to eat!"

(If only Tveritinov wouldn't be too pleased with this idea!) But Tveritinov was delighted and replied, "That would be the greatest kindness on your part! I didn't have the courage to ask."

Zotov turned, looked at the desk, checked the door of the safe, and turned out the light, "Well . . . let's go."

Locking the door, he called to Valya, "If there are any long-distance calls, I'll be back soon."

Tveritinov, in his clownish outfit and his loose, droopy puttees, went out ahead of him.

They walked through a cold, dark corridor, which was illuminated with dim blue lights, onto the loading platform.

Through the darkness of the night, from a sky which they could not make out, swirled a heavy gray cloud of moist flakes that were neither rain nor snow.

The train was standing there on the first track. It was all dark, a little darker even than the sky overhead, so that you had to guess where the cars began or ended. On the left was the engine with its firebox flashing and spewing hot glowing ashes which fell rapidly off on the sides of the roadbed. Still further and higher, as if suspended in mid-air, was a single round green light. To the right, toward the rear of the train, fiery sparks flickered here and there under the cars. Here, in the midst of this life of fire-flashes, dark figures, for the most part old women, were scurrying around the platform. The breathing of these figures flowed together and was made heavy by invisible, cumbersome burdens with which they were loaded. They were carrying children, some crying, some silent. Two of the figures, lugging a large, heavy box between them, bumped into Zotov. Behind them, someone with great difficulty was pulling along the platform a two-wheeled cart with something even heavier in it. (At a time like this, when it was murder to travel — they had to bring along babies and children, and their grandmothers, dragging sacks too heavy to lift, and baskets the size of sofas, and boxes the size of cupboards!)

If there had been no bright, hot cinders under the trains, no semaphores, no flying sparks from the converted cars, no choking flames from the lanterns, no glimmering lights of the trains passing swiftly by on distant tracks, it would have been hard to believe that transport echelons were gathered here. Except for these phenomena the station might have been mistaken for a dense forest, or a dark cleared field undergoing the slow change from fall to winter.

There were many sounds around them: the clanging of chains, the faint horns of the switchmen, the puffing and panting of the trains, the trampling and hubbub of the crowds.

"Here we are!" called Zotov from the passageway at the side of the platform.

He kept moving his wire-meshed lantern from side to side to light Tveritinov's way.

"Oh, something almost tore away my cap!" complained Tveritinov.

The lieutenant walked on in silence.

"All this snow is getting under my collar," Tveritinov continued, trying to keep up this conversation. His coat didn't even have a collar.

"It will be muddy here," warned the lieutenant.

They stepped out into the stickiest, muckiest mud imaginable. There wasn't a dry spot on the road.

"Stop! Who goes there?" The deafening shout of a sentry was heard nearby.

Tveritinov stopped abruptly.

"Lieutenant Zotov!"

Thick, ankle-deep mud sucked at their boots as they went around a wing of the distributing-point building, and up on to the porch on the other side of it. They stamped the mud noisily from their boots, and shook the moisture from their shoulders. Still shining his lantern in the passageways, the lieutenant led Tveritinov into a general, outer guardroom in which stood an empty table and two benches. (The guards of the distributing point ate their meals and otherwise busied themselves here.) They searched for a long time for a cord from which to hang their light. Meanwhile, the unbleached planks of the room were poorly and unevenly illuminated by the lantern which they placed on the bare table. The corners were lost in darkness.

The door of the inner guardroom was opened by the enlisted man on duty. He stood in the doorway, silhouetted against the darkness by the strong electric lights from the inside.

"Where's Guskov?" Zotov demanded vigorously.

"Stop! Who goes there?" bellowed a voice from outside.

Loudly stamping his feet, Guskov arrived on the porch, and hurrying behind him was a Red Army soldier.

"Show yourself, Comrade Lieutenant," Guskov made only a slight motion, somewhat as if he were returning a salute.

In the dim light Zotov noticed an involuntary twitching on

Guskov's face which was always a little sullen and insolent. The twitching was probably the result of the fact that the lieutenant had interrupted him since he hardly ever yielded to him.

Suddenly Zotov shouted angrily, "Sergeant Guskov! How many posts are there in your watch?"

Guskov was not frightened so much as surprised — Zutov never shouted!

He answered quietly, "Two posts — but you know that —"

"I don't know anything! Post yourself, immediately, according to the guard schedule!"

Again Guskov's mouth twitched.

"Red Army Private Bobnev! Take your weapon! Stand at your post!"

The soldier, who had come with Guskov, walked around his leader, stamping heavily on the floor, and went to the designated location nearby.

"And you, sergeant, will go with me to the Commandant."

All of a sudden, Guskov realized that something was wrong.

The Red Army soldier who was carrying a rifle with fixed bayonet, turned, walked briskly past and, at the door of the guard-room, assumed his position.

(And that's when Zotov was seized with uncertainty! The words wouldn't come out the way he wanted them to.)

"You — I — " Zotov spoke very softly, and with great difficulty, raised his eyes to Tveritinov, "— for the time being, I must attend to other matters —" (He particularly and clearly stressed his vowels now.) "— you just sit down here, please, for a little while and wait."

Tveritinov's head looked strange with its wide cap which blended with its fitful shadow cast on the wall and ceiling. His loosely knotted scarf was wrapped around his neck.

"You're leaving me here? But, Vasili Vasilitch, I'll miss my train! You told me to go to the platform!"

"No — No — you stay here —" Zotov hurried to the door.

Then Tveritinov understood and cried out, "You — you're arresting me? What for, Comrade Lieutenant? Please let me catch up with my echelon!"

With the same light movement which he had made when he thanked Zotov, he put his hand to his chest, fingers spread like a fan. He took two quick steps toward the lieutenant, but the alert guard quickly threw his rifle, with its fixed bayonet, in front of him.

In spite of himself Zotov had to look, once more — and for the last time in his life — at the stranger's face in the dim light of the lantern. What he saw was the desperate face of King Lear in these deathly surroundings.

"What are you doing? What are you doing?" cried Tveritinov in a resonant voice. "You know you can never atone for this!"

He thrust up his hands, which seemed to climb out of his short, ill-fitting sleeves. The hand holding his duffel bag caused his black winglike shadow to swell out of proportion, so that the ceiling itself seemed to be pressing down on his head.

"Don't worry — don't worry —," Zotov said, with his foot groping for the threshold of the passageway. "It will only be to clear up one point . . ."

He went out and Guskov followed behind him. As they neared the Army dispatcher's office, the lieutenant said, "Hold this train for awhile."

In his office, he sat at his desk and wrote:

"Operations Center, the NKVD:

Herewith I am sending you a detained straggler who calls himself Tveritinov, Igor Dementevich, who supposedly was left by echelon No. 245413 at Skopin. In conversation with me . . ."

"Get ready!" he said to Guskov. "Take an enlisted man with you and escort the prisoner to the center."

Several days passed, and the holidays ended.

Zotov could not get this man out of his head, this man with his haunting smile, and the snapshot of his young daughter in her striped dress.

Everything, it seemed, had been done as required.

Yes . . . and no.

Either because he wanted to convince himself that the man really was a disguised saboteur or in order to find out whether he had long since been released, Zotov telephoned the junction, to the operations center.

"On the 1st of November, I sent you a detained straggler, Tveritinov. Can you tell me how the case turned out?"

"It's under investigation!" a cold voice answered into the telephone. "But what's the matter with you, Zotov? In your records concerning that cargo which was eighty per cent burned, there's a certain vagueness. This is a very important matter. Someone could be lining his pockets!"

Zotov served as a Commander's Aide at this station the entire winter. Many times he was tempted to call and inquire about Tveritinov, but it would have appeared suspicious.

One day a security investigator from the junction command arrived on some business.

Zotov asked him, casually, "Do you remember a certain Tveritinov? I had him detained sometime last autumn."

"Why do you ask?" the investigator knitted his brows, significantly.

"Just asking . . . I was interested . . . in the outcome."

"We'll take care of your Tveritinov. We never make mistakes."

But afterward, for the rest of his life, Zotov could never forget that man . . .

MATRYONA'S HOUSE

Some one hundred and eighty-four kilometers from Moscow, and a good half year after the incident, all trains slowed down their march almost as if groping. The passengers clung to the windows, went out into the vestibule. Were they repairing the tracks or what? Was the train off schedule?

No. Having gone beyond a crossing, the train picked up speed again and the passengers settled back.

Only the engineers knew and understood what it was all about. And so did I.

1

During the summer of the year 1953, I came back at random from the hot, dusty desertlands — simply to Russia. No one was waiting for me or had invited me anywhere, because I had been detained from returning for a little stretch of ten years. I simply wanted to get back into the heart of the country — out of the heat, into woodlands with rustling leaves. I wanted to cut myself loose and get lost in the innermost heart of Russia — if there were any such thing — and live there.

For a year afterward I might perhaps get a job on this side of the Ural mountains merely pushing a wheelbarrow. Already after considerable construction work had been completed, they had turned me down as an electrician. But I really had a longing to be a teacher. Well-informed people told me that I had wasted my money on the ticket and had stopped there in vain.

But some things were changing already. When I went up the stairway of the District Board of Education and asked where the cadre section was, I noted with astonishment that here the party officials were no longer sitting behind dark leather-upholstered doors, but behind glassy partitions, as in a pharmacy. I went hesitatingly up to one of the little windows, greeted the person on the other side, and inquired, "Tell me, don't you need mathematics teachers somewhere farther along the railroad line? I want to settle there permanently."

They probed through every letter of my personal documents, went from room to room, and called somewhere. For them this was a rare switch — someone asking to get out of the city and into the boondocks. Then suddenly they found a spot for me in Vysokoe Pole [High Fields]. I felt good just hearing the name of the place.

The name did not lie. Set in hills and hollows and then more little knolls, covered with heavily tangled woods, ponds, and embankments, Vysokoe Pole was the one place I was looking for where it would not be an insult to live and to die. There I could sit on a stump in the woods and think for a long time about whatever I wanted to, without worrying about lunch or supper, if only I could remain there and listen at night to the branches rustle in the tree-tops — when the whole world was silent, and not one radio was audible anywhere. But, alas, there was no bread baked there. Nothing edible was sold. The entire village carried its food in bags from the one city in the region.

I returned to the cadre section and made another request at the little window. At first they didn't even want to talk to me. Afterward they all went from room to room, telephoned someone, scratched something with their pens, and stamped my orders: "Torf Produkt" [Peat Products].

Torf Produkt? Ah, Turgenev never knew what such an expression could include.

At the Torf Produkt station, a gray, wooden barracks aging with time, hung the stern warning: "For trains sit only on the waiting-room side"; and scratched with a nail on a board beneath: "And without tickets." But at the ticket window, displaying the same melancholy ingenuity, someone had carved out permanently with a knife: "No tickets." I was to appreciate the precise significance of those additions later. It was easy to arrive at Torf Produkt, but not to leave.

And here in this place had stood, and had remained long after the revolution, thick impenetrable forests. Later they were cut down by the peat exploiters and the neighboring kolkhoz [collective farm]. Its manager, Shashkov, razed quite a few acres of timber and then profitably sold it in the Odessa region.

In the midst of the peaty lowlands the little settlement had grown up haphazardly — monotonous barracks dating from the thirties, and little houses with carved facades and glassed-in verandas, built in the fifties. But one could see that the insides of these little houses were not cut up by partitions reaching up to the ceiling, so that I could not rent a room with four regular walls.

Above the village smoked the factory pipes. Here and there throughout the settlement the narrow-gauge had been extended, and its engines, also belching thick smoke and whistling sharply, drew trains of brown peat, peat slabs, and briquettes. I could assume without error that in the evening over the door of the club the loud-speaker would blare forth, and on the streets drunks would whoop it up a while, not without thrusting at each other with knives.

That was where my dream of a quiet little corner in Russia brought me. But, of course, I could have stayed where I was and lived in an adobe hut, with a view of the desert, with a fresh breeze blowing at night, and the starry vault of the heavens opened wide overhead.

I couldn't sleep on the station benches and at daybreak I strolled through the village again. Now I saw the tiny little market. A solitary woman was there early selling milk. I took a bottle, stood by her, and drank it down at once.

Her speech struck me. It wasn't actually speech, but rather a pleasant singsong. Her words were the kind I had longed to hear, a longing which brought me back from Asia, "Drink! Drink to your heart's content! You dear soul, you're probably a newcomer, aren't you?"

"And where are you from?" I asked, already feeling better. I discovered that not all the inhabitants in the vicinity were peat workers, that behind the railroad was a small hill, and that behind the hill was a village. This village is called Talnovo, and has been there, surrounded by dense forests, since time immemorial, from the days of the former landed gentry. Then follows a whole region of villages — Chashlitsy, Ovintsy, Spudni, Shevertni, Shestimirovo — all deeper in the woods, all a little farther from the railroad and closer to the lakes.

These names drew me like a soothing breeze. They promised me the very core of Russia.

I asked my new acquaintance to take me to Talnovo after the market was over and try to find an *izba* [peasant's hut] where I could find quarters.

It appeared profitable to have me as a tenant. In addition to the rent, the school also promised me a truckload of peat for the winter. The woman's pleasant expression changed to one of concern. There was no place for me at her house (they, she and her husband, were taking care of her aging mother). That's why she took me over to one of her relatives and then to another. But there were no separate rooms at either house, and they were crowded and noisy.

Thus we came to a dammed stream which was drying up and had a little bridge over it. This place caught my fancy more than any other in the village. There were two or three willows, and a crooked little *izba* which leaned far over toward the ground, while ducks were swimming in the pond, and geese, which had gone up the bank, were shaking themselves off.

"Well, perhaps we should call on Matryona," said my guide, already tiring of me. "Only it isn't very clean at her place. She neglects things and is often sick."

Matryona's house was standing there not far distant with four little windows lined up in a cold, ugly wall, its roof shingled on both slopes, and with an ornamented garret window below its tower room. However, the roof was rotting out, the logs of the framework were turning gray with age and although the gate had once been stronger, its pales were thinning out.

The wicket gate was bolted, but my guide did not stop to knock. She slipped her hand under the bottom and turned the latch bolt, a simple device to keep the livestock out. There was no cover over the yard, but most of the house was under one roof. Behind the entrance door an inside stairway rose to a wide landing which was shaded by the roof high overhead. On the left more steps led up to the *gornitza,* a separate structure without any stove, and steps led down to the storage chamber. To the right was the *izba* itself, with garret and cellar.

It had been built long ago and of high quality materials for a large family, but now a solitary woman of sixty lived there.

When I entered the *izba* she was lying down on the Russian stove right there at the entrance, and was covered with nondescript dark rags of the kind which are invaluable in the life of the working-man.

The spacious *izba* and especially the best portion near the windows was strewn with stools and benches on which were earthenware pots and tubs full of rubber plants. They filled the loneliness of the proprietor with a mute but living company. They grew up untrammeled, capturing the feeble light on the north side. In the meager light, the roundish face of the landlady peering behind the stove pipe seemed sallow and sickly in tone. From her eyes which had grown bleary, one could see that illness had exhausted her.

As she talked to me, she was lying up there, face downward on the stove without a pillow, her head toward the door, while I stood beneath. She did not show any enthusiasm at getting a lodger, and complained of the black illness through the paroxysms of which she had just now passed. The illness did not strike her every month but when it did, was so overpowering that, as she said, "For two or three days I won't be able to get up or wait on you. But I'm not particular about the *izba,* and you can live here if you want to."

And she named off for me other landladies where it would be more restful for me, and where I would be more welcome, and sent me round to them. But I had already seen that it was my destiny to lodge in this dimly lit *izba* with its lusterless mirror in which it was quite impossible to see oneself, and, hanging on the wall for decoration, two garish posters brought for a ruble each, one advertising books and the other the harvest.

Matryona made me look elsewhere in the village for quarters, and on my second visit she made long excuses, quoting one of her sayings, "If one neither cleans nor cooks, how can one please?"

Nevertheless she met me standing up, and already something like pleasure struggled to express itself in her eyes because I had returned.

We came to an understanding on the price and on the peat which the school would supply. I learned only later that year after year, for many years, Matryona Vasilyevna had not earned a ruble from any source, because they didn't pay her a pension. Occasionally her relatives helped her out a little. In the kolkhoz she used to work, not for money, but for "credits" in the dog-eared account books.

So I lodged in Matryona's house. We didn't divide off a room. Her bed was near the stove in the corner by the door. I fixed myself a primitive cot by one window, and pushed aside Matryona's beloved rubber trees to set up a small table in the light from another. There was electric lighting in the village — it had already been extended from Shatury in the twenties. At the time, the newspapers wrote about "little Ilyich [Lenin] lamps" and the peasants, their eyes goggling, called them, "The Tsar's lights!"

Perhaps to one of the more wealthy villagers, Matryona's *izba* may not have seemed habitable; nevertheless, for that fall and winter with her it was fine. It still didn't leak from the rains, and the cold winds did not blow the warmth from the stove at once, but only towards morning, especially when it blew from the other side.

Other things lived in the *izba* besides Matryona and myself, such as a cat, mice, and cockroaches.

The cat was elderly, and more important — lame. She had been picked up out of pity by Matryona and had struck roots. Although the cat walked on four legs, she limped badly, and favored one leg, since that foot or leg had been injured. When the cat jumped down from the stove, the sound of her contact with the floor was not a soft feline sound as with other cats, but a powerful, instantaneous strike with the three feet — "toop!" — such a powerful blow that, not being accustomed to it at first I would wince. She placed the three feet together under her in order to protect the fourth.

66

The mice were in the hut but not because the lame cat couldn't cope with them. On the contrary, she sprang at them like lightning from the corner and carried them out in her teeth. But the mice were inaccessible for the cat, because someone in better days had papered the *izba* for Matryona with a figured greenish wallpaper, and not with just one, but with five layers. When these layers stuck together the paper worked fine, but they had peeled from the walls in many places, and formed a sort of internal skin for the hut. Between the wood frame of the *izba* and the skin of the paper the mice had made themselves passages, and rustled about brazenly, as they ran through them even under the ceiling. The cat angrily followed their rustling with her eyes, but was unable to reach them.

Occasionally the cat ate the cockroaches, but they didn't agree with her. The only thing the cockroaches respected was that line of the partition separating the mouth of the Russian stove and the kitchen from the clean area of the hut. They did not creep into this area.

On the other hand, the cockroaches swarmed over the kitchen at night. Whenever I went there for a drink of water late in the evening and turned on the light, the entire floor, the big bench and even the wall were almost solid brown and astir with them. I brought home some borax from the school laboratory and by mixing it with dough, we almost got rid of them. The number of cockroaches decreased, but Matryona was afraid of poisoning the cat along with them. We stopped pouring the poison and the cockroaches multiplied again.

At night when Matryona was already asleep, but I was busy working at the table, the thin, quick pattering of mice under the wallpaper merged with and drowned out the rustle of the cockroaches behind the partition, like the distant sound of the ocean. But I grew accustomed to them. There was nothing evil about either the mice or the cockroaches, and they told no lies. Their rustling was simply for them their life.

And I also became accustomed to the advertising poster beauties which, stuck on the wall, offered me *Belinsky, Panferov,* and reams of other books — only these were silent. I got used to everything in Matryona's hut.

Matryona used to get up between four and five in the morning.

Her clock was twenty-seven years old, and had been purchased at the village store. It was always fast, but Matryona was not worried so long as it did not lose time and make her late in the morning. She would turn on the little lamp behind the kitchen partition, and quietly, courteously, trying not to make any noise, heat up the Russian stove. Then she went to milk the goat (it was all the stock she had, this one, dirty-white, crinkly horned goat). She fetched the water and cooked breakfast in cast-iron pots — one for me, one for herself, and one for the goat.

She brought up potatoes from the cellar — the smallest ones for the goat, little ones for herself, and egg-sized ones for me. As for large potatoes, her sandy garden plot had not been manured since the war and, although she was always planting potatoes, potatoes, and more potatoes, it never produced any big ones.

I hardly heard her bustling about in the morning. I slept long, woke up in the late winter light, stretched myself, and stuck my head out from under the blanket and sheepskin. The latter, plus my prison-camp jacket covering my legs and a sack padded with straw underneath, kept me warm even on those nights when the hard frost from the north pushed through our puny window.

When I heard her restrained clatter behind the partition, I always said in measured tones, "Good morning, Matryona Vasilyevna!"

And she always greeted me from behind the partition with the same kind words which began with a low, warm gurgle of the sort grandmothers make in fairytales: "M-m-mm . . . the same to you!" And a little later, "Your breakfast is ready."

She never announced what was for breakfast, but that was easily figured out: boiled potatoes, or "poh-tah-to" soup (the way everyone in the village pronounced it) or fine-ground barley gruel. That year you couldn't buy any other kind of groats in Torf Produkt except barley, and you had to fight for it at that, because it was the very cheapest, was used to fatten pigs, and was bought by the sackful. Even this was not always salted, as it should have been, was often burnt, and after the meal left a thin coating on the palate and gums, and caused heartburn.

But all that was not Matryona's fault. There was simply no butter in Torf Produkt, the margarine went like hot cakes, and only mixed fats were sold on the free market. Besides, the Russian stove, as I found out, was not suitable for cooking. The cooking took place in the interior hidden from the cook himself. The heat approached the cast-iron pot unevenly. I suppose the stove came down from our ancestors in the Stone Age since once it had been stoked early in the morning, all day long it kept fodder and mash warm for the livestock, and food and water warm for man. It was also warm for sleeping.

I submissively ate everything that was cooked for me, and patiently put aside anything that fell in it and didn't belong, like hair, a bit of peat, or a cockroach leg. I didn't have the heart to scold Matryona.

In any case, she herself always anticipated me by saying, "If one neither cleans nor cooks, how can one please?"

"Thanks," I said, simply.

"For what? Thanks for nothing?" she smiled, disarmingly. And with an ingenuous glance of her faded, pale blue eyes, inquired, "Well, now, what shall I fix you for dinner?"

"For dinner" meant for the evening meal. I ate twice daily, like at the front. What could I order for supper? Always the same thing — potatoes or poh-tah-to soup.

I reconciled myself with this because life had taught me not to consider food the point of daily existence. I placed a higher value on the smile in her roundish face, which I finally tried to capture with a camera, but in vain. When she saw herself in the cold eye of the camera lens, Matryona took on either a strained or an abnormally severe expression. Only once did I get a picture of her as she looked out of the little window toward the street smiling at something.

That fall many injustices were done to Matryona. Her neighbors advised her to try to get her pension. She was all alone and when she became very sick, they had dismissed her from the kolkhoz. Many injustices were heaped on Matryona's head: she was sick, but did not count as an invalid; she had worked for a quarter of a century for the kolkhoz, which, however, was not a factory so the pension was not supposed to be paid out on her account, but on account of her husband, that is, against loss of the breadwinner. But her husband had been dead for twelve years — since the beginning of the war. And now it was not easy for her to obtain certificates from the various places where he had lived, and papers showing how much he had earned. It was a lot of trouble to get these certificates stating that he used to earn at least three hundred rubles a month, testifying that she lived alone, received no help from anyone, and was born in such-and-such a year. Afterward she had to bring all that to the Social Security Office and, having made corrections, discover that it wasn't done that way. So she brought it back again, and tried to find out whether they would give her the pension.

These troubles were made even more difficult by the fact that the Talnov Social Security Office was twenty kilometers to the east, the village Soviet ten kilometers to the west, and the settlement Soviet an hour's walk to the north.

They drove her from office to office for two months — to one for a comma, to another for a period. Each trip meant a day lost. She would arrive one day at the village Soviet, only to find that the Secretary wasn't in, or simply that he was out somewhere in the village. So "come again tomorrow." Now the Secretary is in, but he doesn't have an official stamp. "Come again" a third day. "Come again" a fourth day because, by mistake, they signed the wrong form — Matryona had pinned all the papers together in a single sheaf.

"They're murdering me, Ignatich," she complained to me after such fruitless trips. "I'm worn out with it."

But her face did not remain clouded for long. I observed one thing: she had a sure means of putting herself back into a good mood — work. She immediately either grabbed a shovel and dug up potatoes or, with a sack under her arm, went out to dig peat. Or else, with a wicker basket, she went out to pick berries in the distant woods. Having bent over bushes instead of an office desk, and carrying a back-breaking load, Matryona would return to the *izba* beaming again, satisfied with everything, and with a pleased smile on her face.

Talking about the peat, she said, "Today I struck it rich, Ignatich. I found just the right spot, and now I know where to take it from. It's a pure joy!"

"But, Matryona Vasilyevna, don't you think my peat supply is enough? A whole truckload?"

"Pooh! Your peat! If we had as much as yours and as much again — then, perhaps, there would be enough! When winter strikes and the wind battles at the windows, the heat escapes as fast as you can stoke up the stove. Last summer we laid in a supply of peat by the pile. I would have brought in as much as three truckloads by now if they weren't after us. They've already started to drag one of us old women through the courts!"

Yes, that's the way it was. The frightening breath of winter was already beginning to blow. Excavators growled through the peat bogs, but did not provide peat for the inhabitants, only for the authorities — the teachers, doctors, factory workers — everything for the authorities by the truckload. Fuel was not authorized for Talnov — and no one was supposed to inquire about it. The kolkhoz chairman walked through the village, looked at you with either demanding or ingenuous eyes, and talked about whatever you wanted to except fuel, because he had already laid in a supply for himself. But winter wouldn't wait.

And so, just as they had formerly stolen wood from the landowners, now they hauled off peat from the Trust. The old women gathered together in groups of five or ten to give each other courage. They went during the day. During the summer the peat was piled up everywhere and arranged in stacks for drying. That's the good thing about peat, once dug up it can't be hauled off immediately. They let it dry through the fall and even into winter if the road was not clear. About this time the old women took it. At one stroke they carried away in bags six peat bricks if they were still damp, ten if they were dry. One of these sacks was enough to stoke up the stove once; it had to be carried as far as three kilometers and weighed two poods. [One pood equals about 36 pounds.] There were two hundred days of winter and we had to have heat — in the morning with the Russian stove, in the evening with the tiled "Dutch" stove.

"We've sunk this low!" Matryona exclaimed angrily at some invisible person. "Since we have no more horses, unless you cart stuff home on your own back, you don't have it. My back will never heal. During the winter I pull toboggan loads by myself, during the summer bundles — and that's the God's truth!"

The women went during the day — and not just once. On good days Matryona brought back as many as six bags full. She stacked my peat in the open; hers she hid under the landing, and each evening covered the opening with boards.

"Unless the devils just happen to guess where it is," she said, wiping the sweat off her forehead, "they won't find it for the life of them!"

What could the Trust do? They couldn't free enough staff to post guards all over the peat bogs. Since they had officially reported ample production, they were probably able to write it off as a loss due to crumbling and rains. Occasionally they tried to gather a patrol and catch the women at the entrance to the village. The women threw away their sacks and scattered. At other times, when someone informed, they made a house-to-house search, drew up a report on the stolen peat, and threatened court action. For a while the women would stop bringing peat, but winter approached and drove them to it again — with sleds at night.

Generally speaking, as I got accustomed to Matryona, I observed that, quite apart from cooking and housework, she had to take care of a number of other things every day. She kept the regular order of these things in her head and, rising early in the morning, always knew what she would do. Besides the peat, she collected old stumps wrenched out of the peat bogs by the tractors, and red cowberries which she preserved for the winter in quarter-litre bottles ("Try your teeth on them, Ignatich!" she used to say as she treated me to them). Besides digging potatoes, and running about on account of the pension business, she had to get fodder from somewhere for her one and only, dirty-white goat.

"But why don't you keep a cow, Matryona Vasilyevna?"

"A-ah, Ignatich," explained Matryona, as she stood in her soiled apron at the passageway by the kitchen stove, and turned round toward my table, "the milk from the goat is enough for me. And if I were to get a cow, it would eat me out of house and home. They won't let me mow on the embankment because it belongs to the railway, nor in the woods, which are under the forest service. And since, alas, I'm no longer a member of the kolkhoz, they won't allow me there. All the grass goes to the kolkhoz until late fall, and even the women of the kolkhoz have to scrounge for it after the snow begins. What kind of grass can you find under the snow? In the old days we cut grass from the end of June to the end of July. We used to clear it away — when the meadows were as sweet as honey."

So, gathering grass for her one scraggly goat was hard work for Matryona. She took a sack and a sickle, and went out in the morning to places where she remembered it grew in tufts along the road-side or on islands in the peat bogs. When she had stuffed a sack full of fresh, heavy grass, she dragged it home and spread it out in layers in the courtyard. From each sack she obtained a pitch-fork full of dried fodder.

The new Chairman, recently sent out from the city, cut off the kitchen gardens of all the invalids as his first official act. Fifteen *sotok* [about .37 acre] of sand lot was left Matryona, but ten *sotok* lay idle beyond the fence. On the other hand, when there were not enough hands on the kolkhoz, when the women made really stub-born excuses to get out of work, the Chairman's wife went to see Matryona. She was a city type — determined. She wore a short, gray jacket, and a threatening look, as if she were in the military.

She entered the hut without a greeting and looked sternly at Matryona. The latter was uneasy.

"So-o-o," said the Chairman's wife, dividing the word into syllables for emphasis, "Comrade Matryona, you've got to help at the kolkhoz! You've got to go out tomorrow and haul manure!"

Matryona's countenance took on a half-apologetic smile — as if she were ashamed for the Chairman's wife because the latter would not be able to pay her for the work.

"Well, ah . . . but . . . ," she drew the words out. "After all, I'm sick, and I'm no longer officially a member of the kolkhoz." And then hastily correcting herself, she asked, "What time should I be there?"

"And bring your own pitchfork!" added the Chairman's wife as she went out, her stiff petticoat rustling.

"How about that!" Matryona exclaimed reproachfully afterward.

" 'Bring your own pitchfork!' she says! There's not a shovel or a pitchfork anywhere on the kolkhoz. And I'm living without a man! Who's going to do my planting for me?"

And she pondered over it all evening, "Well, what can you say, Ignatich? After all, they've got to have help — what kind of harvest would there be without manure? And what a hell of a way to run a kolkhoz, anyhow! The women stand around the kolkhoz leaning on their shovels and wait for the factory whistle at noon. Then there's still some business to take care of. The accounts have to be settled as to who came and who didn't. I prefer to work as if there weren't any whistle, only 'oy-oy-oyinki', before you know it, it's evening, and time to fix supper!"

In the morning she went off with her pitchfork.

Not only the kolkhoz, but also a distant, favorite relative or simply a neighbor would come to Matryona in the evening and plead, "Come help me a little while tomorrow, Matryona! We'll dig up some potatoes."

And Matryona couldn't refuse. She abandoned the normal course of her chores, went out to help her neighbor, and returning, would say without envy, "Oh, Ignatich, what big potatoes she has! I dug them up freely. I didn't want to leave that piece of land! And that's the God's truth!"

They never passed over Matryona, especially when it came to plowing anybody's garden plot. The Talnov women had arranged things so that it was harder and took longer for any one of them to dig up her own garden plot with a shovel than if all six harnessed themselves to a wooden plough and tilled the six garden plots collectively. For this reason they called on Matryona for help.

"Well then," it occurred to me to ask one of them, "did you pay Matryona for it?"

For an answer I got, "Oh, she doesn't take any money for it! You have to hide it on her when she's not looking!"

Still another commotion occurred when it was Matryona's turn to feed the goatherds. One of these was healthy, but a deaf mute, and the second was an urchin with a slobbery little cigar stuck between his teeth. Her turn to feed them came around only every six weeks, but it drove Matryona to a great deal of expense. She went to the village store, bought tinned fish, and splurged on sugar and butter, which she never ate herself. It seemed that the women outdid each other trying to see who could feed the goatherds best.

"Everyone is afraid of tailors and goatherds," she explained to me. "They'll give you a bad name all over the neighborhood if something doesn't suit them."

And into this life, already crowded with anxieties, burst periods of serious illness, when Matryona would lie flat on her back for two days and nights without so much as a complaint. On such days Masha, Matryona's closest friend since her earliest childhood, often came over to take care of the goat and to fire the stove. Matryona herself never ate, nor drank, nor asked for anything. To call the doctor from the village medical center to the house would have been unheard of in Talnov. And her neighbors would have thought it inconsiderate — behaving like one of the upper classes. When they did send for the doctor on one occasion, she arrived very annoyed, and ordered Matryona, as soon as she could get up, to come to the medical center. Matryona went, against her will. They put her through various examinations, sent the reports to the regional hospital — and there the matter died. Matryona, herself, was partly to blame.

But her affairs called her back to life. Soon Matryona began to get up, at first moving slowly, but later briskly again.

"You didn't get to see me in the old days, Ignatich," she said, to justify to herself her having been sick. "I could lift any old sack, even one weighing five poods! My father-in-law used to yell, 'Matryona, you'll break your back!' My brother-in-law didn't have to come help me lift logs on the wagon. We had a big, strong horse by the name of Volchek which we got from the military. It was a war horse."

"What do you mean, a war horse?"

"Because, together with the healthy horses which they took to the war, was this wounded one, which they left us. He was a high-spirited animal, and once he pulled our sled into the lake from fright. The men jumped off, but I held on the reins and stood fast, so help me! He was full of oats, that horse. Our men liked to feed horses well. A horse that is full of oats doesn't feel a heavy load."

75

But Matryona was by no means fearless. She was afraid of fires and of lightning, but most of all — no one knows why — of trains.

"Once I rode the train to Cherusti as it came from Nechayevka. Its bright lights blazed and the rails hummed. Ah-h, what a fever it gave me! How my legs shook! — and that's God's truth!" she said, astonished with herself, and shrugged her shoulders.

"You don't suppose you were frightened because you didn't get a ticket, Matryona Vasilyevna?"

"At the little window? They try to shove first-class tickets off on you. But the train was already moving. We dashed here and there saying, 'Please help us!' The men climbed up a ladder onto the top of the car. Then we found an open door and shoved straight ahead without tickets, and the cars were empty, all empty. You could even stretch out on the benches. Why the unfriendly parasites at the window never gave us tickets, I don't know. . ."

Nevertheless, that winter Matryona's life eased as never before. At last they began to pay her a pension of eighty rubles, and she also got a hundred-odd from me and the school.

"Pooh! A fat chance Matryona has of dying now!" some of her neighbors began to say, enviously. "They pay a lot of money to her, the old woman, and she doesn't know what to do with it!"

Matryona had new felt boots made for herself. She bought a new quilted jacket. And she had a coat made out of a railroad worker's leather overcoat, which was given her by an engineer from Cherusti, the husband of Kira, Matryona's foster daughter. A hunch-backed tailor from the village lined it with cloth batting, and Matryona got a nicer coat out of it than she had been able to sew for herself in the sixty years of her life.

In the middle of the winter Matryona sewed two hundred rubles into the lining of the coat for her burial expenses.

For a moment she was happy, "I feel a little better about things, Ignatich."

December passed, and then January — for two months her illness had not struck. In the evening Matryona often went over to Masha's house, sat for a while, and chewed sunflower seeds. Matryona never asked guests over in the evening to her own house out of respect for my work. Only once on Epiphany, when I returned from school, I found people dancing in the *izba,* and was introduced to three of Matryona's own sisters, who, since she was the oldest, called her *nyanya* or *lyolka* [nannie or nurse]. After that occasion, we rarely saw the sisters again. Perhaps they were afraid that Matryona would ask them for help.

Matryona's holiday was clouded by only one event or premonition. She had walked five *versts* [about three miles] to church for holy water, and had set her pot down among the others. When the blessing of water was over, the women rushed in to get it, pushing each other. Matryona was too late to be among the first, and came in at the end. She couldn't find her pot, and no other piece of tinware had been left in exchange for it. The pot had disappeared, as if carried away by an evil spirit.

"Ladies!" Matryona cried, as she walked among the praying women. "Did one of you take, by mistake, somebody else's holy water? In a tin pot?"

No one acknowledged her question. They say that one of the little boys filched it—there were some boys there. Matryona was sad when she returned.

However, this doesn't mean to say that Matryona was a fervent believer. Rather she was superstitious. She was always coming up with superstitions, such as: you shouldn't go into the garden plot during *Ivan Postno* [Lent], otherwise there would be no harvest in the coming year; if the snow whirled during a storm, someone had hung himself somewhere; or, if you pinched your foot in the door, there would be guests. As long as I lived in her house I never saw her pray, and not once did she even cross herself. But all important affairs began with "God bless!" and she insisted on saying "God bless you" every time I left for school. Perhaps she did pray, but gave no sign of it either because she was shy in my presence or feared it might annoy me. There were icons hanging in the hut. On weekdays they were left dark, but at times of vespers and matins, and on the morning of holidays, Matryona used to light icon lamps under them.

Her sins, however, were less than those of her lame cat — the latter throttled mice.

With the past difficulties of her life somewhat eased, Matryona began to stand and listen attentively to my radio on occasion. (I didn't waste any time in turning on the knob — the "kh-nob" as Matryona called it.)

When she heard over the radio that some new machine had been invented, Matryona grumbled from the kitchen, "Always new machines, new machines! They don't want to work with the old ones, but where will they put all of them?"

When they broadcast a report that clouds had been seeded by airplanes, Matryona shook her head over the stove, "Oy-oy-oyinki! They're going to do away with either the winter or the summer!" Once Chaliapin was singing Russian songs. Matryona stood and stood, listening, and then remarked thoughtfully, "He sings strangely, not the way we peasants do."

"But, of course he does, Matryona Vasilyevna, just listen!"

She listened a little while longer, pressed her lips together, and said, "No. That's not it. That's not our way. Besides, his voice quavers."

However, Matryona made up for it. Once they were playing a concert of Glinka's love songs. Suddenly, after the fifth song, Matryona, holding on to her apron, came out from behind the partition, deeply moved. Astonished, she whispered, "Ah, that's it, that's our way!"

2

Thus Matryona became accustomed to me, and I to her, and we got along together. She never annoyed me with questions. Either because she was naturally discreet, or because she lacked the usual curiosity of old women, she never once asked me whether I had been married. All the women of Talnov importuned her with questions trying to find out about me. She always answered them, "If you need to find out something, ask him. I know only one thing about him—he's from far away!"

And when long afterwards I told her that I had done a lot of time in prison, she merely shook her head in silence as if she had earlier suspected as much.

I saw only the present Matryona, failing in her old age, and I in turn did not disturb her past, nor did I imagine that there was much to be searched for in it. I learned that Matryona had been married even before the revolution, right in the same hut in which we were living now, and right "at the oven." (That meant that there were neither mother-in-law, nor older, unmarried sisters-in-law around, and on the first morning of their marriage, Matryona started baking.) I found out that she had had six children, all of whom died, one after another, very early, so that no two were ever alive at the same time. Later, there was a sort of foster daughter, Kira. Matryona's husband never returned from the war, but there had been no death notice. Villagers who had been in his company said that he might have been taken prisoner or killed, but they never found his body. Eight years after the war even Matryona herself decided that he was no longer alive. And it was good that she thought that way — better than if she thought he were still alive and married somewhere — say in Brazil or Australia, and the village of Talnov and the Russian language had been blotted out of his memory.

Once, returning from school, I found a guest in our *izba*. A tall, old man, his hat on his knee, was sitting by the "Dutch" stove on a stool which Matryona had brought out for him into the middle of the room. His entire face was framed with dark hair, which was only lightly touched with gray. A thick dark mustache blended into his broad beard so that his mouth was barely visible. Continuous dark sideburns, almost concealing his ears, merged into his dark, matted, drooping hair. His even broader, dark eyebrows grew together like a bridge. The bald dome of his forehead blended into the hairless top of the skull. The entire appearance of the old man indicated great wisdom and dignity. He sat stiffly, his hands folded on top of his staff, which was resting plumb with the floor. He sat in an attitude of patient expectation, and it was evident that he had hardly spoken to Matryona who was busy behind the partition.

When I came in, he slowly turned his majestic head toward me and addressed me suddenly, "My dear fellow! . . . I can't see you clearly. My son is a pupil of yours — Grigoriev, Antoshka."

He wouldn't have had to say anything more. Along with my

impulse to help this venerable old man, I knew in advance and rejected all the useless things he was now about to say. Antoshka Grigoriev was a round-faced, high-colored stripling in the eighth grade, with a look like a cat that had finished off a canary. He came to school as if he were on a holiday, sat over on one side, and smiled lazily. Moreover, he never prepared his lessons at home. But, most importantly, the schools of our district, province, and neighboring provinces were noted for passing a high percentage of students. For this reason he was passed year after year. He clearly understood that no matter how much his teachers might threaten him, he would pass anyway at the end of the year, so there was no need to study. He simply laughed at us. He sat in the eighth grade, although he had never mastered fractions, and couldn't tell one triangle from another. For the first two quarters he had a hard struggle with failing grades, and the same fate awaited him during the third quarter.

The half-blind old man looked more like Antoshka's grandfather than his real father. He came to me humbly, his hat in his hand as they would say today, to complain. How could I tell him that the school had been deceiving him year after year? That this could go on no longer, otherwise the whole class would go to pieces, and would turn into chatterboxes? If I did so, I would be reflecting unfavorably on my work and on my own prestige as a teacher.

So I patiently explained to him that his son had been badly neglected, that he lied both at school and at home, and that he should check on the boy's grade book more often. The boy should be taken severely in hand by both of us.

"But, my dear fellow, I've already roughed him up," my guest confirmed. "I already beat him once a week, and I have a heavy hand!"

During the conversation I recalled Matryona herself had once interceded for Antoshka Grigoriev. At the time I hadn't asked whether he was a relative of hers and declined to do what she requested. Matryona stood at the kitchen door, a silent suppliant on this occasion too.

When Faddei Mironovich left, saying that he would call and check up on things again, I said, "I don't understand, Matryona Vasilyevna, how Antoshka is related to you."

"He's the son of my brother-in-law," Matryona answered stiffly, and went out to milk the goat.

When I had figured it out, I realized that this dark, persistent old man was the brother of her husband who had disappeared without a trace.

The long evening passed. Matryona didn't refer to the afternoon's conversation again. Only late in the evening when I had forgotten about the old man and was working in the quiet of the hut to the rustle of the cockroaches and the ticking of the clock, suddenly from the darkness of her corner Matryona said, "Once upon a time, Ignatich, I almost married him."

I had forgotten about Matryona herself, that she was there, and didn't hear her, but she spoke out of the darkness in agitated tones, as if the old man were still wooing her. Obviously, that was all Matryona had thought about all evening.

She got up from her wretched, raggedy bed, and slowly came toward me, as if she were following her own words. I leaned back and for the first time saw Matryona in an entirely new light. There was no overhead light in our room as it was filled with a forest of rubber trees. From a table lamp the light fell in a circle only on my notebooks. To eyes distracted by this light, all the rest of the room appeared in rose-colored semidarkness. Out of this darkness Matryona came forward. For a moment I imagined that her cheeks were not yellow as usual, but rose-colored instead.

"He proposed to me first . . . even before Yefim . . . He was his older brother . . . I was nineteen, Faddei twenty-three. They lived right here in this very house. It was their house. Their father built it."

I involuntarily looked around me. Suddenly throughout the old, gray, rotting house with its two faded-green skins under which the mice were running, oozed the cheery, resinous smell of fresh pine logs, as yet undarkened, still unplaned.

"And you . . . loved him? Well, and then what?"

"It was during that summer. We went for a walk and sat down in the grove," she said in a whisper. "There was a grove there where the stables are now. They've since cut it down. I almost got married, Ignatich, but war with the Germans was beginning, and they took Faddei off to the war."

81

As her words fell, there flashed before me the deep white and yellow July of the year 1914 — a peaceful sky, drifting clouds and people bustling about in the ripe stubble. I pictured them beside each other — he a black-haired Hercules with a scythe over his shoulder, and she, a blushing girl with her arms around a sheaf of wheat. And there was singing, singing under the open sky the way people no longer sing in this machine age.

"He went off to war — and fell. For three long years I kept silent and waited, but not a line, not a word from him."

Matryona's senile, roundish face, wrapped in a faded little shawl, looked at me in the soft, indirect light of the lamp. It seemed suddenly detached from her everyday, slipshod dress, and free from wrinkles, like the face of a frightened young maiden before a terrible choice.

"Yes, yes . . . I remember . . . The leaves were flying everywhere; the snow fell—and later melted. They ploughed again, they sowed again, and again they wept. Once more the leaves were flying, and again the snow fell. Then came one revolution; then another, and the world turned upside down. Their mother died, and Yefim asked me to marry him. He said, 'If you want to come to our house, then come and live with me.' Yefim was a year younger than I. We have a saying: 'The wise girl marries after Michaelmas Day [in the fall] — the fool after St. Peter's Day [June 29th]!' They didn't have enough hands at their house, so I came to them. The marriage ceremony took place on St. Peter's Day, and on St. Nicholas' Day that winter, Faddei returned . . . from a Hungarian prison camp."

Matryona closed her eyes. I kept silent.

She turned toward the door, and spoke excitedly, "He was standing on the threshold. How could I shut him out? I wanted to throw myself at his feet! But that was forbidden . . . 'Well,' he said, 'if Yefim weren't my own brother, I'd cut you both down with this axe!' "

I shuddered. I could vividly imagine her anguish and fear, as he stood there, dark, in the shadow of the door, and threatened Matryona with his axe.

But she quieted down, and leaning on the back of the chair in

82

front of her, continued in a singsong voice, "Oy-oy-oyinki, the poor dear man! There were so many girls in the village, but he married none of them! Faddei said, 'I shall look for another Matryona to take your place!' So he married Matryona from Lipovka. They built a separate log *izba* for themselves where they are living now. You pass by their place every day as you walk to school."

Oh! So that was it! Now I realized that I had seen the second Matryona more than once. I didn't like her. She was always coming over to my own Matryona to complain that her husband beat her, that he was niggardly, and that he was working her to death. She would cry for hours, and her voice was always full of tears. But it turned out that my Matryona had nothing to regret. Faddei had always been that way to his own Matryona all his life and had always kept a heavy hand on the entire household.

Speaking of Yefim the old woman continued, "He never once beat me. He used to take after men on the street with his fists, but not once after me. What I mean is, there was one time when I had been quarreling a while with my sister-in-law, when he smashed a wooden spoon on my forehead. I jumped up from the table and shouted, 'I hope you choke to death, you drones.' I ran off in the woods and he never touched me again!"

It appears that Faddei had no reason to complain. His second Matryona had borne him six children and they all survived. Among them was my Antoshka; he was the youngest, the runt. But no children remained to Yefim and Matryona — they never lived as long as three months, and though none was sick, each died.

"I remember one little daughter, Elena, when she had only just been born. They had just washed her body when, as she was lying there, she died. That spared the washing of the dead body. Just as my wedding was on St. Peter's Day, so I buried my sixth child, Alexander, on St. Peter's Day."

So the whole village decided that Matryona was "hexed."

"A hex on me?!" Matryona shook her head with conviction. "They took me to a woman who used to be a nun, for treatment. She poured something down my throat and waited for me to cough out the hex, like a frog. Well, nothing ever came out!"

Years passed, like water flowing. On the forty-first [in 1941] they didn't take Faddei for the war because of his poor sight. However, they did take Yefim away. And like the older brother in the first war, the younger one vanished in the second. And this one really didn't return. The once noisy but now deserted *izba* was rotting away and advancing in years, and growing old within it was Matryona, forgotten and abandoned.

So she asked the second Matryona—whom everybody persecuted —for her youngest daughter, Kira, for a child of her womb (or was it a spot of Faddei's blood she wanted?)

For ten years Matryona took care of Kira like one of her own children who never survived. And not too long before I came she had given her in marriage to a young railroad engineer from Cherusti. Recently she had been getting a little help from Cherusti, occasionally sugar, or when a pig was slaughtered, some of the fat. Since she was suffering from ailments and expected her death in the near future, Matryona announced her will. After her death the separate wood frame of the big room, the *gornitza,* which was connected with her *izba,* was to be given as a legacy to Kira. She said nothing at all about the *izba* itself, and her three sisters still hoped to get hold of it.

Thus, it was on that evening that Matryona completely opened up her heart to me. And it so happened, as the connections and meaning of her life had been made somewhat clear to me—during those very days—things started moving. First, Kira arrived from Cherusti, and the old man, Faddei, became worried. It seemed that in Cherusti the young couple would have to put up some kind of a dwelling in order to obtain and hold a plot of land. The *gornitza,* that is, the wood frame of Matryona's house, was just right for this purpose. There was no way to put up another, be- cause they couldn't get hold of the wood for it anywhere. Not only Kira and her husband, but especially old Faddei, were eager to get that strip of land in Cherusti.

So Faddei became a constant visitor at our house. He came again and again, spoke to Matryona in an authoritative tone, and demanded that she give away the *gornitza,* immediately, while she was still living. On these visits he did not give the appearance

84

of an old man, leaning on a cane, who might fall to pieces at the first shove or harsh word. Although he was slightly hunched over with backache from disease, this impressive old man, more than sixty years old, who had kept his hair lush, dark and youthful, pressed his claim hard, and with fervor.

Matryona didn't sleep for two nights. It was not easy for her to make up her mind. She didn't mind giving up the empty *gornitza,* since it wasn't being used anyway, just as she had never minded giving her care, work, and property to others. In any case the *gornitza* had been willed to Kira. But she was terrified at the idea of tearing down the roof under which she had lived for forty years. Although I was only a tenant, even I felt sick at the thought of their tearing off the boards and pulling out the logs of the house. And, for Matryona, it would mean the end of everything.

But the others insisted on it and knew that Matryona's house would have to be torn apart while she was still living.

One February morning Faddei arrived with his sons and sons-in-law, and the five of them began working with their axes, setting up a squealing and creaking as they ripped off the boards. Faddei's eyes flashed with businesslike efficiency. In spite of the fact that his back would not straighten out entirely, he climbed dexterously up under the rafters, and bustled vigorously about, shouting occasionally for helpers. As a little boy he himself had helped his father build the house. That *gornitza* belonged to him, the eldest son, and had been put up so that he might move in with his bride. Now he was feverishly tearing the *gornitza* apart, to carry it away from Matryona's yard. After numbering the logs and marking the ceiling boards, they dismantled the *gornitza,* including the storeroom underneath. The *izba* itself, with what was left of the landing, they boarded up with a thin, temporary wall. They left chinks in the wall, and everything indicated that they were wrecking the place, not building it, and that they did not suppose Matryona would be living there much longer.

While the men were breaking things up, the women were making home-brew for the day of loading. They made their own liquor because it would have been too expensive to pass vodka around. For the makings, Kira brought a pood of sugar from the Moscow district, while Matryona Vasilyevna, under cover of the night, carried over the sugar and the bottles for the home-brew.

The logs were carried off and stacked outside the fence, ready for the engineer to arrive with the tractor from Cherusti.

On the same day a heavy snowstorm began — a "blower" as Matryona called it. It howled and whirled for two days and nights piling huge snowdrifts on the road. Afterwards, when the road had just been treaded down, another truck would drive past. Then there was a sudden warm spell, and in one day everything thawed at once. A gray fog formed; streams broke through the snow and babbled forth; and you got stuck up to the top of your knee-boots.

For two weeks the tractors couldn't reach the disassembled *gornitza*. These were two weeks of perplexity for Matryona. One of the heaviest burdens she had to bear was her three sisters, who came over and with one voice called her a fool for giving the *gornitza* away; they said they never wanted to see her again, and then left.

On the same day the lame cat ran out of the courtyard and disappeared. The first event went with the other. This also depressed Matryona.

Finally the road, which had been melting away, was hardened by frost. A sunny day came, warming the heart. Matryona had had pleasant dreams the night before. In the morning she learned that I wanted to take a photograph of someone standing beside one of the old-fashioned looms which remained in two *izbas* in the village, and which had been used to weave coarse rugs.

Bashfully, and smiling ironically, she said, "Why not wait a little, a couple of days, Ignatich, until they take away the *gornitza*, and snap the picture then? I'll put up my own loom; I've still got it, and that's the God's truth!"

Clearly, she liked to picture herself in an old-fashioned setting. The red, frosty sun flooded everything with an almost rose-colored light. As it streamed through the frost-covered window of the enclosed passageway, which had been partly cut down, this light cast a warm glow over Matryona's face. Such people always

86

have fine faces, in tune with their consciences.

Later, as I was returning from school, just before twilight, I saw movement around our house. A big new tractor-drawn sledge was already loaded with logs. But there was no room for a lot of the timbers, so the family of old Faddei, and others who had been invited to help, had nearly finished knocking together a second homemade sledge. All were working like mad, almost with desperation, as is so often the case with people who have caught the scent of big money, or who anticipate an orgy of food and drink. They were yelling at one another, and arguing among themselves.

The argument was about how the sleds should be pulled — separately or together. One of Faddei's sons, who was lame, and the son-in-law engineer kept harping that they shouldn't try both sleds at once, because the tractor couldn't pull them. But the tractor driver, a lusty, self-opinionated, bull-faced lout, shouted that it was obvious that he was the driver, and that he would pull both sleds together. His calculation was clear — according to the plan, the engineer would pay him for the transportation of the *gornitza*, not by the trip. Two trips in a single night were out of the question. It was twenty-five kilometers each way and one return journey. And by morning he had to be back with his tractor in the garage from which he had secretly taken it for this job on the side.

The old man, Faddei, couldn't bear not to move the whole *gornitza* in one day, and so motioned to his sons to give in. The second sled, put together in a slapdash fashion, was hooked on to the stronger one.

Matryona ran among the men, bustling about, and helping roll the logs on the sledges. I then noticed that she was wearing my quilted coat. She had already smeared the sleeves with icy mud from the logs, and I spoke to her about it with displeasure. I had a sentimental attachment to that padded coat; it had kept me warm during my troubled years.

And so for the first time I got angry at Matryona Vasilyevna.

"Oy-oy-oyinki, my poor old head!" she exclaimed, taken aback. "Why, I simply grabbed it on the run and forgot it was yours! I'm sorry, Ignatich."

And taking it off, she hung it up to dry.

The loading was finished and all who had been working, about ten men in all, thundered past my table, and dived behind the kitchen curtain. There was a muffled clinking of glasses. Occasionally a bottle tinkled. The voices grew louder, bragging and laughing. The tractor driver was especially boastful. The heavy odor of home-brew rolled toward me.

But they didn't spend much time drinking — the darkness compelled them to hurry. They began to leave. Self-confident, with a brutal face, the tractor driver left first, and then, in order to accompany the sleds to Cherusti, the engineer son-in-law, Faddei's lame son, and one of the nephews. The rest of them dispersed and went home. Faddei, brandishing his staff, hurried to catch up with someone and set him straight about something. The lame son lingered at my table for a smoke, and suddenly began to speak, telling me that he loved Aunt Matryona, that he had recently gotten married, and that his wife had just given birth to a son. Then the others called him, and he left. Through the window I heard the tractor roaring.

Last of all, Matryona darted hastily out from behind the partition. She shook her head anxiously at those who had gone. She was wearing her quilted coat, and had put on a shawl.

From the doorway she said, "Why didn't they reckon on two tractors? If one broke down, then the other could pull the load. But what will happen now — God only knows!"

And she ran off after the others.

After the drinking, the arguments, and the departure, it was especially quiet in the abandoned *izba,* which was chilled from the frequently opened door. Outside the windows it was quite dark. I also put on a quilted jacket, and sat down to check over some examination papers. The tractor could no longer be heard in the distance.

An hour passed; another, and then a third. Matryona had not returned, but then I wasn't surprised. After seeing the sledges off, she must have gone over to see her friend, Masha.

Another hour passed, and still another. It was not only dark, but a sort of deep quiet prevailed. At that time I didn't grasp the reason for this stillness, or why, as it happened, during the whole evening not one train passed by on the tracks, which were about a third of a mile away from the house. My radio was silent, and I noticed how much — more than ever before — the mice were romping, how impudently and noisily they ran around under the wallpaper, squeaking and scraping.

I fell asleep and when I awoke, it was one o'clock in the morning and Matryona had not yet returned. Suddenly I heard several loud voices from the direction of the village. Although they were still distant, something told me they were coming to the house. And sure enough, soon a sharp knock sounded at the gate. A powerful, strange voice shouted for me to open up. I went out with a flashlight into the pitch darkness. The village was sound asleep. There wasn't a light visible in any window. Even the snow, which had started melting in the past week, reflected no light. I turned the lower night latch and let them in. Four men in greatcoats entered. A very unpleasant sensation that — when men burst into your house at night, noisily, and in greatcoats.

I examined them in the light, however, and recognized that two of the men in the overcoats were railroad officials.

The elder, a heavy-set man with a face like that of the tractor driver, asked, "Where's the owner, the old lady?"

"I don't know."

"Did the tractor with the sledge leave from this courtyard?"

"From this one."

"Were they drinking here before leaving?"

All four were looking around and screwing up their eyes in the half-light from the table lamp. I realized that either they had already arrested someone, or wanted to make an arrest.

"Why, what happened?"

"Answer our questions!"

"But. . ."

"Did they go away drunk? Were they drinking here?"

Had they killed someone? Or was it forbidden to carry away the *gornitza*? They were pressing me very hard. Only one thing was clear: Matryona might have to do time for making the home-brew. I stepped back toward the partition and thus screened off the kitchen area.

89

"I really didn't notice. I didn't see anything."

(I actually hadn't seen anything — I had only heard.)

And as if perplexed, I gestured with my hands, indicating the furnishings in the hut: the peaceful light of the table lamp on the books and notebooks, the crowd of startled rubber plants, the severe cot of an anchorite — no trace of debauchery.

Then they themselves disappointedly observed that there hadn't been any kind of carousing going on. They turned to go out, saying among themselves that even if a drinking bout had not taken place in the *izba,* it would be a good idea to report that it had. I followed them, and tried to find out what had happened.

Only when he reached the wicket gate, one of them growled at me, "It raised hell with all of 'em. They can't even pick up the pieces!"

Another added, "But that's a small detail. The one o'clock express nearly jumped the track — that's what happened!"

And they all left hurriedly.

Stunned, I turned back into the hut. Who were "all of 'em?" Where was Matryona? I drew aside the kitchen screen. The stench of home-brew struck me. The place was a shambles — tables and benches overturned, empty bottles lying around, one of them half-empty, glasses, half-finished herring, onions and sliced fat pork.

Everything seemed dead, except for the cockroaches crawling undisturbed on their battlefield.

They had said something about the one o'clock express. Why? Perhaps I should have showed them all that mess behind the screen. I still had my doubts about the whole business. But what kind of damned manners did they have? Not to explain anything except to officials!

Suddenly our wicket gate squeaked, and I quickly ran out toward the bridge. "Is that you, Matryona Vasilyevna?"

The door to the courtyard opened.

Wringing her hands and unsteady on her feet, Matryona's friend, Masha, entered the house.

"Matryona. . . Our Matryona, Ignatich!"

I had her sit down, and, hampered by her tears, she told the story.

90

At the railroad crossing there was a little hill after a steep approach. There was no barrier. The tractor had pulled the first sled across when the rope broke and the second sled, the homemade one, got stuck and began falling to pieces. (Faddei had provided inferior wood for it, for the second sled, that is.) The tractor driver and Faddei's lame son managed to pull the first sledge a little way off, and had returned to the second. They were splicing the rope when Matryona — heaven knows what brought her there — rushed in between the tractor and the sledge.

Now how did she expect to help the men? She was perpetually getting herself mixed up in men's affairs, such as the time at the lake when a horse almost knocked her down through a hole in the ice. And why did she go to the damned crossing anyhow? She had already given away the *gornitza*, and all her debts had been settled. The engineer kept looking to make sure that the train from Cherusti didn't appear suddenly. He could have seen the lights in the distance. But from the other direction, from our station, two engines coupled together came up — without lights and moving backward. Why they were running without lights nobody knows. When an engine backs up, coal dust pours into the engineer's eyes from the tender so that he can't see very well. They came flying up, and crushed to a pulp the three people who were between the tractor and the sledge. The tractor was wrecked, one sledge was split into kindling wood, the tracks were thrown off the ramp, and both engines turned over on one side.

"But why didn't they hear the engines coming?"

"Because the tractor ahead of them drowned out the noise!"

"And what about the dead bodies?"

"They won't permit anyone to touch them. They've roped off the area."

"But what was it I heard about the express? Was there one?"

"The ten o'clock express was already moving out of our station and toward the crossing. But when the engines crashed, the two engineers weren't hurt. They jumped free, ran back down the tracks waving their hands, and managed to stop the train."

The nephew was hit by a log which rolled acrossed the tracks.

He hid out at Klavka's house, so that no one would know that he too was at the crossing. Otherwise he would be dragged into court as a witness. As the Russian proverb puts it: "The one who sleeps on the stove never gets bothered — the others all get caught!"

"Kira's husband got off without a scratch. He tried to hang himself, but they pulled him out of the noose. 'Because of me,' he says, 'my aunt and brother were killed!' Then he went and had himself arrested. But now instead of going to jail, he'll go to the insane asylum. Oh, Matryona, my dear little Matryona!"

Matryona was no more. Someone close to me had been killed — and only the day before I had reproached her for wearing my quilted coat! From the book advertising poster on the wall, the reddish-yellow figure of a woman continued smiling happily.

Old Masha sat a while longer and continued to cry.

When she rose to leave she suddenly inquired, "Ignatich! You remember? Matryona had a large gray knitted shawl . . . She really intended it after her death for my daughter, Tanya, right?"

She looked at me hopefully through the half-darkness. Was it possible that I had forgotten? But, no, I remembered.

"Right — she really had intended it for Tanya."

"Then look here! Maybe you won't mind if I take it with me right now? Tomorrow the whole family will come flying over, and afterward, it'll be too late for me to get it!"

Again she looked at me hopefully, pleading — this friend of Matryona's for half a century — the only one in all the village who really loved her. Surely she deserved it.

"All right — take it!" I confirmed.

She opened the small trunk, took the shawl, thrust it under her skirt, and left.

Some sort of madness had seized the mice. They were running so furiously up and down the walls that the green wallpaper seemed to move in almost visible waves over their backs.

In the morning I had to go to school. It was three a.m. There was nothing left for me to do except to bolt the door, and lie down to sleep.

Lock the door because Matryona wasn't coming back!

I left the light on and lay down. The mice were squeaking

92

— almost groaning — and running — running all over the place. I had to rid my tired, incoherent mind of an involuntary anxiety — a feeling that Matryona had returned invisibly to say farewell to her house. And suddenly in the darkness on the path in front of the entrance, I imagined that I saw the young, dark-haired Faddei with his axe raised, "If he weren't my own brother, I'd cut you both to pieces!"

Forty years had flown by since his threat had been made from the corner there. The threat had hung like an old broadsword — which had struck at last!

3

At daybreak the women, using a sled, brought back all that remained of Matryona, which had been covered with a dirty sack. They took off the sack in order to wash her. Everything was jumbled together. The feet, half of the trunk, and the left hand were missing.

One of the women said, "God left her little right hand so that she can cross herself where she's going!"

The whole crowd of rubber plants which Matryona had loved, was taken out of the *izba*. She had loved them so much that once when she had been awakened in the night by smoke, she didn't rush to save the *izba*, but to turn the plants over on the floor so they wouldn't suffocate. The floors were swept clean. They curtained over Matryona's lusterless mirror with a wide towel of old, homemade cloth. They snatched the cheerful posters from the walls. They moved my table. On stools by the window, under the icon, they set the plain, unadorned coffin, which had been hastily knocked together.

Matryona lay in the coffin. Her lifeless, mangled body was neatly and simply covered with a clean sheet. Her head was enveloped in a white kerchief, but her face, undamaged and peaceful, seemed more alive than dead.

The villagers came to stand around for a while and have a look. The women brought their children to stare at the deceased. When anyone began to cry, the women, as if obliged to do so — even if they had come out of empty curiosity — all stood around the walls and the door and wept as if they were an accompanying chorus. But the men stood silently at attention, their caps in their hands.

It fell to the lot of the relatives to do most of the mourning. I observed in the weeping a coldly thought-out, ages-old established order. Those who were somewhat distant relatives came up to the coffin for a short while and lamented softly over it. Those who considered themselves part of the dead woman's family began weeping while still on the pathway, and having reached the coffin, bent down and wailed in the face of the deceased. There was a different, home-made melody for each mourner, and each set forth her own thoughts and feelings.

Then I realized that the mourning over the deceased was not simply mourning, but a kind of political contest in its own right. The three sisters had flown in together. They had seized Matryona's *izba,* her goat, and the stove. They had closed the trunk and locked it. They had also dug the two hundred rubles saved for burial expenses out of the lining of Matryona's coat. They tried to prove to all who came that they alone were the closest to Matryona.

Over the coffin they mourned, "Ah, *nanya, nanya*! Ah, *lyolka, lyolka*! And to think you could have lived so quietly, so peacefully! And we would always have taken such tender care of you! Oh, why did your *gornitza* lead to your destruction? The cursed *gornitza* dealt a final blow to you! Why did they break up your things? And why didn't you listen to us?"

The laments of the sisters were indictments of Matryona's husband's family. Obviously they were meant to prove that there was no need to break up Matryona's *gornitza*. While the underlying thought was: "The men have grabbed the *gornitza* and we're not about to give up the *izba* itself!"

The husband's family, Matryona's sisters-in-law (i.e., the sisters of Yefim and Faddei) and a few assorted nieces, then went up to the coffin and mourned in this fashion: "Ah, auntie, little auntie! Why didn't you guard yourself against them? And now they most likely take offense at us! To think that *you,* our dear relative, that it was all your fault! And the *gornitza* had nothing to do with it! But why did you go there, where death rubbed you out? No one

94

called you there! And the way you died! Unthinkable! Why didn't you listen to us?" And behind all this lamentation the real reason stood out clearly: "We're not responsible for her death, and we're still going to talk about who gets the *izba!*"

By then the gross, broad-faced "second" Matryona, the substitute Matryona whom Faddei had taken only because of her name, had gotten into the contest, wailing simple-mindedly, and crying hysterically over the coffin: "Yes, you there, my darling little sister! Is it possible that you could take offense at me? There was a time when we two talked and talked together. Please forgive me, a poor, unfortunate creature! Oh-ma! You went to your dear mother, and surely you will return for me, too! Oh-ma-ah!"

With that "Oh-ma-ah" she literally exhausted all her breath, and began beating, beating her breast against the side of the coffin.

Then, since her wailing had exceeded the accepted norm, all the other women, as if they recognized that her mourning had succeeded only too well, advised in a friendly tone, "Cease! Cease!"

Matryona stopped, and afterward went up and sobbed again, even more fervently. Then an old woman from the village came out of the corner.

She placed her hand on Matryona's shoulder and said solemnly, "There are two riddles in this world: How I was born — I don't remember; how I shall die — I don't know!"

Matryona fell silent at once, as did all the others, so that there was an interlude of absolute quiet.

But this same old woman, who was much older than all the others present, and almost a total stranger to Matryona, after a brief interlude, also wailed, "Oh, you, my poor sick one! Oh, you, my Vasilyevna! Oh, I'm growing tired of saying farewell to all of you!"

And somewhat unusually, with the plain sobbing characteristic of our own age (which has had plenty of practice at it), the ill-starred Kira wept — Kira, Matryona's adopted daughter from Cherusti, for whom they had broken up the *gornitza* and moved it away. Her wavy curls were pitifully disarrayed. Her eyes were red, as if they had been wiped with blood. She didn't notice that her scarf had slipped to one side in the frosty air and her coat sleeves hung down past her arms. Beside herself, she had gone from the coffin of her foster mother in one house to the coffin of her brother in another. They also feared for her reason because her husband would have to stand trial as well.

It appeared her husband was guilty on two counts — he not only removed the *gornitza,* but he was also a railroad engineer, who knew the regulations about unguarded railroad crossings, and should have gone to the station to give advance notice about the tractor. A thousand human beings were on the Urals express that night, sleeping on upper and lower benches in the half-light shed by the train's lamps. They could have all been killed! Back of the whole affair was the greediness of a few people to get hold of a strip of land, or to spare the expense of making a second trip with the tractor. And behind all that was the *gornitza,* on which a curse had lain ever since Faddei's hands had seized and broken it up.

As for the tractor driver, he was already beyond human justice. But the railroad administration itself was also guilty because they had not guarded the busy intersection, and because the coupled engines were running without lights. That was why they tried to switch the blame on the drinking, and then to keep the case out of court.

The rails and roadbed were so badly torn up that for the three days during which the coffins rested in their respective houses, the trains did not run. They were rerouted on another branch line. All Friday, Saturday, and Sunday, from the end of the inquest to the burial, the tracks were repaired night and day. The repair crew were freezing. For warmth by day and for light at night, they built a fire out of the boards and logs which they picked up for free from the second sled, scattered near the crossing.

But the first sled, loaded and intact, stood not far from the crossing and it was precisely this which tormented the soul of the dark-bearded Faddei all day Saturday. One sledge was waiting there with its ropes ready, teasing him, and perhaps Faddeus might still save the second from the fire. His daughter's mind was disturbed, and the outcome of the trial hung over his son-in-law. In his own house lay his son, killed by himself on the same street on which he had killed the woman he once loved. Faddei had come and stood by the coffin, clutching his beard, but not for long.

His high forehead was clouded by painful thoughts, but the thoughts were about how to save the logs of the *gornitza* from the fire and from the crafty designs of Matryona's sisters.

As I thought about the townspeople of Talnov, I realized that Faddei was not the only one in the village with such thoughts.

As for our property — either personal, or the people's — it is strange that the language calls it "goods." And yet losing any of it would be considered disgraceful and stupid by the people!

Faddei rushed about, now in the settlement, then at the station, from authority to authority, without stopping to take a seat anywhere. Capitalizing on his back, which he couldn't straighten up, and leaning on his staff, he asked each authority to make allowance for his old age and to decide that the *gornitza* should be given back to him.

Someone handed down a decision in his favor. Faddei gathered together his surviving sons, sons-in-law, and nephews, borrowed horses from the kolkhoz, and hauled back the remains of the *gornitza* into his own yard along a winding road which passed through three villages. He completed the job during Saturday night and Sunday.

The burial took place on Sunday. The two coffins met and went down the center of the village, with the relatives quarreling over which coffin should go first. Afterward the old woman and her nephew were placed in a single, wheeled *rozvalni* [a sort of wide sledge]. Over the February snow crust, which had recently thawed, under a cloudy sky, they brought the deceased to the church graveyard, which was two villages away from us. The weather was windy, very unpleasant, and the priest with his deacons waited in the church without going out to Talnov to meet them.

The people followed slowly to the edge of the village and sang in chorus. Afterwards they fell back.

The bustling of the old women had not quieted down even on Sunday evening. One old woman purred the psalter over the coffin. Matryona's sisters scurried around the Russian stove with the oven prongs. Out of the mouth of the stove blazed heat from the peat which had been fired up—peat which Matryona had brought in a sack from a distant bog. Using some wretched flour, they baked tasteless patties.

It was already getting on toward evening when they returned from the burial and gathered for the funeral banquet. They seized the tables, putting them in line in the place where the coffin had been that morning. First they all stood around the table and an old man, husband of the sister-in-law, read aloud the Lord's Prayer. Then they poured out for each of us just enough honey and hot water to cover the bottom of a small wooden bowl. Using spoons, we ate this slowly without anything to go with it. Afterward we ate a little something, drank vodka, and the conversation became livelier. Before eating the *kissel* [a jellylike oatmeal porridge] we all rose and sang "Eternal Memory." (They explained to me that it was obligatory to sing this song before eating the *kissel*.) There was more drinking, and the talk became even louder, but it was not about Matryona at all.

The husband of the sister-in-law boasted wildly, "Did you notice, orthodox believers, that the funeral service was conducted slowly today? That's because Father Mikhail noticed me. He knows that I know the service. Otherwise he would only have waved the incense censer, and, 'Saints defend us, homeward wend us,' that would have been the end of it!"

At last the supper ended. Again all rose and sang, "She is worthy!"

And again, with three repetitions, they sang, "Eternal Memory." But the voices wheezed, and were discordant. Their faces were drunk, and no one put much feeling into this "Eternal Memory."

Afterward, the special guests left and only the nearest relatives remained. They pulled out their cigarettes and smoked, laughing and joking.

There was some mention of Matryona's husband, who had disappeared without a trace. The sister's-in-law husband, beating his breast, assured me and the bootmaker, who was married to one of Matryona's sisters, "Yefim died! He died, I tell you! Otherwise why couldn't he come back? Why even if I knew they would hang me when I returned to my native land, I'd come back all the same!"

The bootmaker nodded his head in agreement. He had been a deserter who had never left his native land at all. He had spent the entire war at his mother's house, hiding in the cellar.

High on the stove, getting ready to spend the night, sat that stern silent old woman, more ancient than all the ancients. She looked down from above in mute disapproval of the boisterous, unseemly conduct of the fifty- and sixty-year-old young people.

Only the unfortunate foster daughter, who had grown up within those walls, slipped behind the partition and wept.

Faddei did not attend Matryona's funeral supper because he held one of his own for his son. But during the next few days he aggressively entered the hut twice for talks with Matryona's sisters and the bootmaker-deserter.

A quarrel began over the *izba*—over whom it belonged to, to the sisters or the foster daughter. They almost took the case to the law court but came to a reconciliation, having decided that the court would give the *izba* away to neither of them, but to the village Soviet. They made a deal. One of the sisters was allotted the goat, and the *izba* went to the bootmaker and his wife. In figuring Faddei's share, since, as he said, he "had raised every little log with his own hands," the *gornitza*, which had already been hauled away, went to him. They also let him have the shed where the goat lived, and the whole of the inner fence between the yard and the garden plot.

And once more, although a prey to infirmities and rheumatic pains, the grasping old man revived, and became young again for a while. Once more he gathered together his remaining sons and brothers-in-law. They dismantled the shed and the fence, and he himself hauled away the logs on little sleds, one after another, with only little Antoshka from the eighth grade to help him towards the end — only on this job he couldn't dawdle.

They boarded up Matryona's *izba* until spring, and I moved in with one of the sisters-in-law, not far away. On various occasions this sister-in-law recalled things about Matryona, and enlightened me on new facets of the dead woman's character.

"Yefim didn't really love her. He used to say, 'I like to dress up, like quality folks, but she dresses any old way, and always looks like a hick. Well,' he says, 'in that case she doesn't need anything,' and he began to squander their savings on drink. One time we drove to the city with him, looking for work. Yefim had acquired a mistress there, and he didn't feel like coming back to Matryona."

All her references to Matryona were disparaging—she was slovenly—she didn't care about material things—she was not thrifty—she didn't even keep a suckling pig. For some unknown reason, she didn't like to fatten them. Also she wasn't very smart because she helped other people without getting paid for it. (And indeed, there was cause for her to remember Matryona, because now she could no longer call on her to pull the plough in her garden plot.)

Even Matryona's warmth and simplicity, which her sister-in-law acknowledged, she spoke about with scornful pity.

And it was only thus—through these disparaging comments of her sister-in-law—that an image of Matryona emerged, one which I had never fully grasped while we were still living side by side.

And indeed! Every *izba* had its suckling pig — but Matryona's house had none. What can be simpler than to feed a greedy piglet which cares for nothing in the world except food? What could be simpler than to warm its swill three times a day, to live for it, and afterwards to cut its throat and have the fat back?

But Matryona never had it.

She never tried to acquire things for herself. She wouldn't struggle to buy things which would then mean more to her than life itself. All her life she never tried to dress smartly in the kind of clothes which embellish cripples and disguise evildoers.

She was misunderstood and abandoned by her husband, having buried six of his children. Her moral and ethical standards made her a misfit. She was considered "odd" by her sisters and her sisters-in-law—a laughingstock—because, as they said, she was so stupid as to work for others without pay. She never accumulated property against the time of her death when her only possessions were a dirty-white goat, a crippled cat, and rubber plants . . .

We all lived beside her, and never understood that she was that righteous one without whom, according to the proverb, no village can stand.

Nor any city.

Nor our whole land.

100

"The slow unfolding of Matryona's life and character, her fortitude, kindness, and sudden flashes of humor and wisdom put this story right next to the best Russian peasant scenes written by Turgenev or Tolstoy."
— Ernest S. Pisko in
Christian Science Monitor

" 'Matryona's House' is brief but stunning in its impact, a portrait of a woman and of an age; warmth, humor and tenderness ultimately fuse in a tragic vision that makes the author comparable with Tolstoy and Turgenev."
—Ernst Pawel in *The Nation*

"This is a delightful little book containing two of this outstanding young Russian author's first short novels. They show the same deep perception and tender feelings that the author exhibited in *The Inner Circle* and *The Cancer Ward.*"
— Bart Lanier Stafford, III, in *El Paso Times*

". . . two artful, moving novellas. . . . Both stories are significant examples of the 'new look'—rebellious and idealistic—in current Soviet literature."
— *Library Journal*

"If the tale of Lt. Zotov is testimony to the author's power to deal with complex human problems as well as political ones, Matryona's shows us the pitch of his song. The ending has symphonic force. . . .
"In Matryona the narrator has found his Russia. In Solzhenitsyn, I think, Russia may have found her twentieth-century Turgenev, her twentieth-century Chekhov."
— Robert Maurer in
New York Herald-Tribune

". . . doubt has lingered whether Solzhenitsyn's talent might not be more political than literary.
"These doubts have been smashed with the publication of two more equally short, dry, sharply etched and deeply humanistic stories. . . ."
— Harrison E. Salisbury in *New York Times*